CAMOUFLAGE
RØMILLY KING

The Teams
Book One

CAMOUFLAGE

First edition. December 1, 2022.

Copyright © 2022 Romilly King.

ISBN: 979-8215776339

Written by Romilly King.

Chapter One

Camo

"I would know that walk anywhere." Ethan is laid out naked on the bed, one arm behind his head, his elegant body all gleaming skin and fascinating muscles.

"Yeah?" I say, because I'm a smooth son of a gun.

"The way you move, it changes," he says, "When you're in the mood. When you want to play."

Play is Ethan's way of saying '*When you want to rail me into the mattress.*' That's my husband, always the nice boy, even using euphemisms when it is the right time to talk dirty.

Fortunately I don't have a problem verbalising what I want from him right now.

"Present that ass for me." My voice is low and growling and I see goosebumps break out on his skin. With effortless grace he rolls onto his front and goes up on his hands and knees, arching his back. His build is slight but beautifully toned. He is limber and flexible from all the yoga he does. He says he does it for peace of mind, I don't care, it makes his body perfect for me.

The low light makes his red hair seem darker, like a rain drenched fox, and his pale skin is scattered with cinnamon freckles as if someone dredged him in spice just for me.

God, I love this man.

I love that he responds so truthfully to me, his expressions so open and real, his body vibrating like a tuning fork when I touch him.

I love that I can excite him just by ordering him around, just by giving him a glimpse of the alpha version of me.

He is everything I ever wanted.

I slide onto the bed behind, my thick thighs pressed up against his lean ones. My hands almost cover his ass. I spread his cheeks and

1

look down at him, his skin is shiny with lube. Ever pragmatic it looks like Ethan has prepared himself for me. He doesn't want it drawn out tonight, he wants the full man in charge experience. Fine by me.

He shivers with need as I blow on his hole.

"Gonna make you feel this until I come back." I tell him.

"Want to."

He gasps when I press a finger into him. He's soft and ready, slick inside. I could have just slid into him even though I'm on the larger size. I think he wanted that. I do like to tease him though.

I roll the pad of my finger over his prostate and he jerks, whimpering.

I slide another finger in and he eases his thighs further apart, his back bowing into a deeper arch.

He comes apart so honestly for me. He always did. His responses are so open, he never holds back.

He's begging by the time I slide my cock into him and when I settle deep inside him his whole body is shivering.

I want more of his skin against mine.

I hold him back against me and his arms come up, reaching around the back of my head, scratching at the close cropped hair, as if he is trying to hold on. He whines as I slowly rotate my hips and I bite the side of his neck, "Shh, angel, you don't want to wake Felix." The bite makes him vibrate. "You wouldn't want our son to see what a little slut his Daddy can be for me." That makes him groan. He does love it when I call him that.

I run my hands up his firm chest, the skin like silk under my fingers. His nipples are hard and pebbled. I tweak them gently. "Wanna get deep inside you sweetheart, want to fuck you all the way to your heart."

I sink to my side, pulling him with me. Inside him my cock is squeezed by the elastic strength of his muscles. I moan into his hair as I arrange him on his side and lever his leg up so I can fuck him deeper. He turns his head and looks up at me, his eyes glassy with desire and pleasure, his skin flushed from his cheeks to his chest. He seems so small as I curl around him but his frame hides a tensile power honed by years of yoga. I get an arm under his thigh, open him up even more and drive into him.

His eyelids flutter and he bites his lip, holding in his cries. As soon as I get back from this next mission I'm taking him somewhere, just the two of us, where he can be as noisy as he wants to be.

"Going to come on my cock?" His pale cock, rising from the thick dark red patch of hair that fascinates me, leaks onto his six pack.

He can barely speak, his mouth open, panting, desperate. "Yes, please make me."

My own orgasm is so close I am hanging on by my fingernails, my balls pulled up tight, sheer willpower holding it back.

I slam into him and grind myself inside the pliable heat of his body and he throws his head back. I feel his pleasure like a hot fist clamping around me. He groans, almost a sob and his cock jerks against his belly, spilling creamy liquid.

I let go and my orgasm seems to go on and on. I hold him hard against me, lost in the scent of him, the feel of him, the ongoing joy of him.

Gradually our breaths slow. I slide out of him and he makes a little noise of loss. "Greedy," I say, and he rolls towards me, a dopey smile on his face.

"I'm about to enter the deep sea famine season, don't know when I will get it again."

"I don't think this will be a long trip," I tell him, "Hopefully."

I settle onto my back and he maneuvers himself up against me, his body tucked against me, his head on my shoulder.

The room is warm and calming, all pale colours and mellow wood, a real reflection of Ethan, from the limed wood of the closet doors to the big old antique bed with the four barley twist posts. I bask in the moment, looking up at the rafters and the reclaimed wood light fitting with the thick scrolled arms. The candle bulbs are turned to a low glow. I feel like I could drop off to sleep but I want to stay in the moment a little longer.

Ethan's warm breath fans across my chest and I have one bulky arm wrapped around him, toying with the necklace he wears. It's a little golden starfish on a chain from Tiffany. I bought it for him as a joke after I realised just how serious I was about him. I just love his starfish! I bring him starfish themed presents back from overseas. It's one of those stupid in jokes that couples have, and it never gets old. Being in love should mean you get to be as silly as you like.

"I shouldn't complain about you having to go away. I get the best of both worlds," Ethan's head is warm and solid on my chest, "I get the dreamy guy who grows orchids, regular honeymoons when you come home, and when you let loose I get the big bad Alpha."

"And I get to play with your starfish."

"If only you had a decent sense of humour it would be perfect."

"Shut up, or I'll spank you."

"Promises, promises." I can hear the smile in his voice.

Our bodies fit comfortably together, long practice making this home.

"Caribbean again?" he asks.

"Yeah. Won't be a long dive, just a survey I gather."

"Try and get some sun this time," he strokes his hand over my chest, "You came back from the last trip looking like you'd been in the Arctic!"

I hadn't been in the Arctic, but I hadn't been in the Caribbean either. I really needed to keep my geography straight but that role had been a rushed job.

"Not a lot of sunlight inside a metal tube with four other guys."

"I don't know how you do it."

"I'm a very compartmentalised man."

He tweaks a nipple, but gently. "And still not funny."

It's the truth though. I am. I'm the most compartmentalised man I know. I love him to death, but the moment I walk out of here I'm a different man, with a different role and I have no problem doing it.

Ethan thinks I'm a commercial diver taking on saturation diving projects all over the world. Actually I'm the leader of a team of covert operatives working on top secret missions worldwide.

Ethan calls me Cameron. My team calls me Camo. I'm the alpha in front, wrangling a group of men who do bad things for good reasons.

My cover as a diver is seamless. It explains the travel, it explains being out of touch, it explains the occasional injuries, and god knows it is as dangerous as my real job.

It's a cunning camouflage, it's my way of making me invisible to the rest of the world. It works, and I get the best of both worlds. I get to be the me that gets off on the adrenalin, and then I get to come home and slip into this camouflage and the hot body of the man beside me, and go unseen.

I guess I need him, more than he needs me. He's my camouflage as much as I am his husband.

"Take care, keep breathing down there," he says quietly, like he does every time before I leave.

"Always, every breath brings me closer to being back here with you and Felix," I give him my usual reply.

I mean it, just not quite in the way he thinks, and that's fine. What he doesn't know can't hurt him. This little ritual of ours, it's familiar and it's loving, just because what he thinks it means, and what I think it means, are different, doesn't change anything.

Ethan

I wake to an empty bed and my body aching in all the right places. I also wake to the smell of pancakes.

It's a tradition, Cameron makes pancakes on the mornings he has to leave. It's good for Felix who likes his routines, and it helps us all deal with the regular partings.

From his first days in a house with two Dads Felix knew pancakes made by Cameron meant one Dad was going away, but that he would come back.

Felix doesn't handle change well. Not with his background. He's actually my nephew. I adopted him around the time Cameron and I got together, when everything seemed to be happening at once, as often happens in life. I was falling in love with Cameron, changing my physiotherapy practice to work with having a young traumatised child to look after, and mourning the needless death of my sister.

Alice died of a drug overdose. Felix was locked in with her dead body for three days. He was two at the time. He's just six now. He's small for his age, has a touch of asthma, tends to disassociate when he gets stressed, and goes to regular therapy sessions that we intend to keep up forever. He still has occasional nightmares that he can't talk about, but generally he's a happy little boy, with a quiet stoicism and a love of gardening - mainly thanks to the ongoing influence of Cameron, Mr Big Bad Flower Lover.

My body protests the vigour with which I roll out of bed. Damn, he railed me into the mattress last night. I grin at the memory; nothing beats waking up smug knowing you drove a man wild with desire.

I take a quick shower and pull on some yoga pants and a soft tshirt before making my way downstairs as fast as my poor abused body will let me.

"Pulled a muscle, baby?" Cameron is standing behind the kitchen counter, spatula in hand, muscles on display, and a cocky grin on his face.

"Just a little stiff this morning," I say, and press a kiss to his bare bicep, just above the astronaut tattoo that floats there, as I attempt to saunter past.

"Really," he says, eyebrow raised, "Do you need help dealing with that before Stat picks me up?"

"It'll wait until you get back," I tell him archly.

Felix, sitting at the counter, focussed on inhaling pancakes, doesn't even glance at us. Cameron and I grin at each other like the idiots in love we still are after two years married.

I pour myself a mug of coffee and slide, somewhat gingerly, onto the stool next to Felix. "Sleep okay, small child?" I ask him, dropping a kiss of his hair. It's dark red, like mine, like Alice's was, we're a gene pool full of redheads.

"Yeah. Can I have one more pancake?"

"Hell, yes you can, I need to feed you full of pancakes so you can dive with me as soon as you are old enough." Not waiting for my answer Cameron slips another pancake onto his plate, and Felix flashes him a smile.

I glance at the door, Cameron's well travelled green canvas kit bag is already there along with his smaller backpack. "Early start?" I ask.

He nods, "Stat should be here soon, he's picking me up, and he'll drop me back afterwards, save you having to come get me."

I nod silently, the impending sense of separation starting to settle in. I take a sip of my coffee. Cameron flips a pancake, trying to make me smile. I dutifully dredge one up for him. He knows it takes effort.

I am determined not to be down in front of Felix, we try to make his second Dad's regular departures no big deal even though it is hard.

Felix heads upstairs to finish getting ready for school and Cameron finishes off the pancakes.

When the doorbell sounds Cameron goes to let Stat in and I flex my shoulders, trying to release the tension I can feel creeping in. I'll try to fit in some meditation after I drop Felix off at school or I'll be useless for my patients, they need me loose and relaxed to properly implement the adjustments they need.

"Hey Husband of my Leader, how are you?" Stat says as he follows Cameron over to the breakfast counter.

Stat is such a sweet guy, all eager and boyish despite the killer bod and the megawatt smile. He is like a California sunrise on this misty eastern seaboard.

I love to tease him. He has the most adorable blush.

"I'm good, sweetheart," I tell him, "Wishing it was me that was going to be locked in a tin can with your hotness for a few days." He blushes, all rosy gold.

"Don't bug him," Cameron growls, "And I can assure you the hottest thing about him is the gas he produces." He glares at Stat. "You had better not have eaten any Mexican in the last few days, those refried beans nearly had us putting you out the airlock last time."

"It's why nobody has ever made a porno starring sat divers, it's the least sexy environment there is - five guys in a tin can, a long way underwater."

"I'd give it a good try," I wink at Stat. "And I bet you sound hot as hell with your voice all squeaky from the gases," I say to my husband because he did make me feel good last night, and he gets pouty if left out of the flirting.

"Don't you know it!"

I can see Cameron is itching to go. He hates goodbyes, and so do I, it's why I try so hard to keep it light.

Felix comes downstairs, his school bag over his shoulder. "Hello, Stat," he says politely.

"Can I borrow one of your Dad's for a little while?" Stat asks him.

Felix appears to consider it. "Which one do you want?"

"Can I have the smaller one? He takes up less room."

Felix smiles, "I think you had better take the bigger one. The smaller one will be lost in the diving gear."

"Oh funny," I comment.

"He has a point," Stat says, "Diving equipment is pricey, and as we've plumped for the giant economy size I guess we'll have to stick with it."

"Go kiss your Dad goodbye," I tell Felix quietly.

He makes short work of it, hugging Cameron swiftly and pressing his smaller face to Cameron's short beard. "See ya, Dad," he whispers.

He bolts out to the car and I grab my keys and follow him. I turn back to glance at Cameron, I want to kiss him until I run out of breath but that always makes it worse.

Instead I let my eyes tell him how I feel.

I miss you.

Don't leave me alone.

Come back soon.

All the things I don't say out loud because they aren't fair.

He nods, I know he hears the thoughts, marriage does that, it lets you hear the unspoken stuff.

Chapter Two

Camo

I sling my kit bag in the back of Stat's blue truck and climb into the cab. The sun shines on the white siding and mellow brick of my home and I'm glad I found time to cut the lawns yesterday. I hope Ethan remembers to check the greenhouse is doing it's thing, I'd hate the baby orchids to suffer in my absence.

Everything looks neat and normal and tidily civilised, from the bright blue shutters on the window to the raised vegetable beds down one side of the yard.

Time to leave it all behind.

Stat starts the engine and I slip off my wedding ring, tucking it into the small pocket on the side of my back pack and cinching the strap that holds it closed tight. I pat it fondly.

"Does it bother you?" Stat asks. He doesn't look at me, instead focusing on the road as he pulls out of the drive.

"What, leaving?"

"Leaving, and lying."

"No," I say, "It never has. Lots of people work away, and everybody lies about something."

"I suppose," he agrees with a shrug.

He doesn't know, he hasn't got a partner, he's young and free and single. At least I think he is. Stat might be the closest to me of my team, and the only one that ever comes to my home, but I'm not even sure of his orientation, let alone if he has someone serious.

We don't really talk about personal stuff. For some of us it's a real issue, and the only triggers we need to pull are the ones on our weapons, so we steer clear of certain topics.

I suppose I could ask him, Stat is the most normal of my team. He was a Witness back in the days of the Handler system. And he was a good one, a real asset. He speaks several languages, he's an expert with computers, and despite a quirky sense of humour he's calm and stable. He might not be as deadly as the others but his stocky build has its fair share of muscles, and he isn't afraid to get his hands bloody.

Stat, which is short for his Team name of Static, is our communication specialist, he's our front runner and rear guard, he's the one that gets us in and gets us out.

With his blonde hair, blue eyes and a ready smile he gives the impression of being good looking but harmless to everyone he meets. Ethan thinks he is adorable. I think he is damn good at his job, and it doesn't make me nervous to have him interact with my family. I can't say the same about the others.

"Any idea what the role is?" I ask.

"All I know is Edwards says it is going to be a fast in and out and it's Caribbean based. Could be drugs, could be people trafficking."

"Keeping it close to his chest as usual," I say, "He really does like the whole secret mission thing."

"Yeah, but despite the eyepatch he ain't no Fury," says Static, "and we're not Agents of Shield."

I grin and settle back in the seat as we drive north out of Rockville, heading towards Frederick and the 120 acres of pasture, woods and streams that we work from.

We call our base The Farm, mainly because the CIA call their clandestine operations training centre the same thing, but our base actually is a farm. We like to think we're the real thing in all ways.

Stat keeps up a stream of chat as we head up I270, turning off at Ballenger Creek. I think he thinks it helps me switch roles. I don't disabuse him of the idea but I don't need it. The minute I get in the cab of the truck everything switches, but I still need to get my head around herding the unherdable.

I wrangle a team of the least likely to cooperate, and sometimes I wonder who the hell thought this was a good idea. Then I remember that the world is a messy and terrible place, for women, for the sexually diverse, for all the minorities and the inherently powerless, the poor and the weak, and we're here to give them a chance. That's always going to be a good idea.

That's how I see our work.

In the dying days of the Handler system it became obvious that those who worked in the program, the trained killers, the nimble minded witnesses, and the rugged support staff were not all going to go quietly into the sunset. Turns out not everybody wanted us to.

We were all assets in one way or another, we should have seen it a mile off that when one system ended we would be wanted by another, equally painted in shades of grey.

When the idea of The Teams was first pitched to me it focussed on the reality that we were a set of diverse individuals that were used to working together. Certain of us would struggle to find gainful employment in other spheres because our work environment had conditioned us to a particular set of circumstances. The Teams was an offering of continued income to people not designed to be in the mainstream.

I got that straight away. Hell, even though I had started dating Ethan I couldn't see myself settling into the kind of work that brought me home every night and kept me bored. I felt that although I was pushing forty I was in my prime, and I wanted a job that would keep the old adrenaline drip feeding my alphaness.

My cover story as a diver was already established with Ethan, it was a no brainer to consider a move to the new organisation, and then Edwards sold me on the details.

I wasn't being offered a supporting role, I was going to be leading a team, from the front, in the thick of the action. This wasn't about mopping up the dregs a Handler left behind, or extracting one after a cock up.

The Teams was the Handler and Witness system ramped up to the next level. All the assets working together with the same goal in mind.

I trusted Edwards, he had been an exemplary operational head in the Handler system, and I wanted to carry on working with him. If anyone could make this new thing work it was him. He had experience across the board of Handlers, Witnesses and Support Staff. Being hand picked by him to join The Teams was something I wish I could have boasted to Ethan about.

We're two years into this now. We're not perfect but we've gone through shakedown and my team is settled - two former handlers, a former witness and two former support staff. We're not the well oiled machine we could be, but I think we'll get there. The psych tests say we're a good fit, we just need to get over the teething difficulties.

The motivation is there to make it work. I'm optimistic about that because I believe what we are doing is right.

Edwards put it best when he said "When men of goodwill are willing to get around a table and talk, change has a chance to happen. We clear the path to that table."

I believe we can negotiate our way to a better world because most people are decent. If only the right people get to be in charge.

That's what we do. We do dirty jobs to ensure that in the near future the people most likely to negotiate are put in a position to negotiate.

We exist to give the world a chance to heal.

The Teams have taken out dictators, threats to democratic elections, religious fundamentalists, and the heads of certain corporations. People who were either stopping good change happening, or refusing to negotiate to allow change, or who were implementing changes that would set the development of a decent society back. We have rescued whistle blowers, retrieved documents, helped activists get out of countries trying to kill them.

I think we do good. I know we do good.

Our roles come from beyond these borders, from beyond this government. Only Edwards knows for sure where the word comes from but the role always matters. On the rare occasions when we brush up against other agencies they seem to know who we are. The technical backup we receive is excellent.

The only problem, if we get caught, there is no way out. Nobody will be coming to save us. We'll go down as nameless mercenaries for an unknown master. That's fine. We all take that risk, and we make sure to not get caught.

Stat slows the truck and turns off the road at a large metal gate. It begins to open as he makes the turn, picking up the transmitter on his vehicle.

The main building is a long low barn like structure housing an open plan workout room and chill out room, a separate kitchen, a formal briefing room where the computers are, and a mezzanine level with rooms we bunk in if we are staying on site.

Stat lives at The Farm, close to his beloved computer array and constantly in touch with Janus, our intelligence contact. Edwards has an office here, and we have a shooting range and an armoury built into outbuildings. The rest of the land is given over to a few home pastures for the look of it, deciduous woodland and ridiculously scenic streams. If it wasn't for the guns and psychopaths it's the kind of place you would want to raise a family.

I know there are several other bases like this but I have no idea where they are and no interest in finding out.

"Did Snipe come in with Berk?" I ask as I spot Berk's truck parked next to Blue's hybrid.

"Yes, they were both in town."

Snipe is our sharp shooter, hence his code name. He's probably the most unstable of the team on paper.

The code names are there to help us feel part of a team and to protect us. Who we really are and what we once were doesn't have a place in this environment. Edwards and I know everything that it is necessary for us to know about the team, but what they choose to share with each other is entirely up to them.

It makes sense to me. It saves preconceptions.

That said, Snipe is definitely the most volatile of the group, until you put a gun in his hand, then he is totally focussed. He can shoot the tail feathers off a hawk at half a mile. He was the last of the Handlers to take active service and he made ten kills in his first year. He is utterly ruthless and very driven because if he stops the rage comes, and that's not good for him.

He was an abused child; nameless, beaten, bounced around the foster system. The only thing that saved him from a life of crime was his self awareness and his intelligence. He walked into the offices of the Handler system when he was 21 years old and said "Take me in." He went through the training in under six months. He is a killing machine with an attachment disorder. I didn't want him on the team initially but he fitted in with the others. He's not a true psychopath but he is a very damaged man.

Blue on the other hand is the real deal. He's a psychopath from the tips of his toes to the ends of his dark blonde hair - tastefully styled. Codename Blueprint, he's our logistics expert.

In the field he is whatever he needs to be, a total chameleon, outside of action he is quiet, very controlled, highly organised. He knows his ability to function depends on self control and routines. I consider him solid in the field because of his background and his training.

If there was blue blood in the Handler system he would be it, brother to Nathan Jones, former head of the Handler system, and brother in law to the legendary Handler Gray he was raised in the system and then received additional mentoring from his extremely wealthy and utterly lethal brother in law.

Blue is elegant, well mannered, fits in anywhere, and he could kill you in the blink of an eye and make it look like art. He's a valuable asset, but I wouldn't want him too close.

Other than Stat nobody comes to my home, not ever Berk, our muscle man, and he's neurologically normal.

I drag my kit out of the truck and follow Stat into the main building. Blue is working out with Berk, the two of them moving together in sync on a training mat as they go through Tai Chi moves that look like dancing and need muscles of steel.

Berk and I should bond, he's ex military, like me, built like a brick shit house, like me, and yet I can't connect with him. Maybe it's the vegan new age thing he has going on. Berk is big into waving crystals around. He has mandalas tattooed on the back of his hands. Off duty he wants nothing more than to discover inner peace. I think he's trying to find where his soul went because in the field he's a machine, no fear, and very gung ho. Holding him back can be hard.

Edwards opens the door of his office, "Briefing in five," he says.

"Let me grab a coffee," I reply, and head into the kitchen.

Snipe is cleaning his favourite rifle on the industrial metal table that we eat at. We nod to each other and I pour myself some coffee that looks like sump oil.

Felix will be in school now, Ethan will be with his first patient, I'm about to find out who we're going to kill next, and why.

Briefing takes place at the kitchen table after Snipe has stowed the rifle, it's less formal than our official briefing room.

We all have coffee when Edwards strides in.

"Gentlemen," he greets us, and then nods towards Blue, "Indigo."

"It's Blue, Sir, not Indigo" I remind Edwards, but I do it respectfully, I look up to the man.

He ignores me.

"How is Trans?" Edwards asks.

"Thriving," Blue says, and his usual coolness fades for a moment. "Get's bored when I'm not there though."

"Naturally," Edwards says, and I can tell he wants to say more but knowing Blue as well as he does doesn't mean he can bring it up here, that makes us all uncomfortable.

"You have a role for us, Sir?" I bring him back on track.

Edwards drags his eyes away from Blue. He seems tired. I would too if I just sat behind a desk. It's the field that gives men like us energy.

In the language of The Teams - as carefully constructed as that of the Handler system - a "*role*" is a job, a mission, a case. It's something that needs our particular skills.

We're not just wet work, despite what some of our former colleagues think and we don't take on every role that is offered to us, hence the briefing.

This is the role, as Edwards lays it out.

The nicely placed Caribbean island of Concord is a fledgling democracy in the middle of an election that could send it sliding back to the bad old days. Once a haven for drug runners and the modern pirates of the Caribbean it has taken huge strides in the last decade under the care of a President not out to line his own pockets.

Median income is up, social standards are rising, unemployment is falling and money flowing in is staying in country.

That could all change.

The election is proving to be the testing ground for all that is bad about misinformation in the digital age. Someone has paid a lot of money to swing it and the contender, old school, moneyed, schion of a family with a familiar name, is ahead in the polls. For no good reason and a lot of bad ones.

Concord, is the poster child for first world influence. Everything has been on the up since the President came to power and there has been no oil involved! Always a plus.

Concord does have strategic importance on fighting the war on drugs, it's on the sea route north from the coke fields, but more than that it's home to a burgeoning computer hardware industry with investment bringing high tech jobs that have altered the economy for the better. That is the main reason we want to keep it democratic, to keep that hardware investment safe in western hands. And the people deserve it. Between hurricanes, disease and earthquakes they had a shitty 20th century. They deserve the changes that have come recently.

The role we are being asked to take in this is to remove the contender in the election, one August Brown.

He has been groomed for this run for the presidency, it's been a long time coming. Unfriendly influences have thrown a lot of money at this, we believe because of the ability to gain access to a high tech manufacturing base in a western friendly country. However, he is one man, if he was removed this disinformation campaign would flounder with no candidate to rally behind and the current President would get at least one more term to consolidate the gains made.

We are being asked to, if possible, make this look like a robbery gone wrong, or an accident.

What is your opinion on the role, gentlemen?

"How long do we have to consider the role?" I ask.

We've made the acceptance of the roles we are offered into a ritual. It's a protocol we developed right at the start of running The Teams - the role has to be acceptable to our moral code.

It doesn't have to be white hats all the way, but it has to make sense to our somewhat twisted sense of justice. We were never saints, but we all chose this work. Choice is important to us, we want what we do to mean something.

One thing we really don't do is only what a government wants, any government. Elected officials come and go, none of them particularly care, so don't bother putting something you can brag about politically in front of The Teams, the answer will be no.

"You have a couple of hours, but time is of the essence, the election is heating up, now is the best time to act." Edwards says.

"Do you have anything more to add?" Blue asks, "It seems somewhat tenuous for us. We need to be sure this is not a vendetta hit."

"This is about mass manipulation at heart," Edwards says, "If we don't do this, those who manipulate elections, those who sway under-educated populations with misinformation get another win. They have won too many lately, we need to show them we are watching."

"Countries get the governments they deserve." Snipe speaks up.

"They did, now they are subjected to incessant misinformation and targeted manipulation so they choose the government someone paid for."

"So this is all about democracy? Want us to go in with flags on our backs, showing our allegiance?" Berk is being provocative, they all are, they like this part of the process, it makes them feel validated, and who doesn't like that.

"None of us here are huge fans of democracy," Blue's voice is a lazy drawl, "We don't really drink the kool aid on that."

"This isn't about democracy," Edwards' expression shows what he thinks of that construct. "This is about people having access to information in order to make informed choices because now, more than ever, knowledge is power."

"What are the alternatives to an assassination?" Stat asks. He always wants to know if there is another way, a better way. "Can he not just be persuaded to stand down? Does this have to be a kill?"

"That route was tried numerous times when this problem was first anticipated. We saw this problem coming a while ago but we didn't expect to see such resources thrown at it. It seems the candidate is less the organ grinder, more the monkey in this. The show is being run by his illegitimate brother. We believe the brother fed certain proclivities of the candidate who is now totally under his command."

"If he is a victim of his brother then surely retrieving him would be a more humane option."

"Oh, he's not whiter than white, he isn't the victim here, he has some revolting traits of his own but they don't factor in the kill order unless you want to hear them. If you require further information whilst you consider the role then you may consult with Janus, or make your own enquiries."

Janus is our intelligence expert. He's only available to us via voice over internet. We've never met him and have no idea who he is. Stat named him Janus because he's always looking through doors. Stat is normally the one to speak to him, the rest of us seem to piss him off for some reason.

After Edwards leaves the room I send Stat to consult with Janus, he returns in twenty minutes looking faintly sick.

"I'd have ordered a kill on August Brown based purely on what he does in his spare time," he says, "Guy is scum, any Handler would have taken one look and started to prepare the courtroom. Frankly, with his tastes, if he gets into power his private parties will make Saddam Hussein look like Santa Claus."

"That's good enough for me," Snipe says.

"Anything is good enough for you," Berk says.

"Fuck off," says Snipe, but without heat.

"I've also got the fake news articles and the micro targeting profiles they are using to inflame conflicting factions within the population." Stat pushes some papers across the table to us. "They are aggressively looking to drum up internal tensions that have been quiet for a decade. Janus also suspects they will nationalise the tech enterprises if they win and have China come in to oversee the operation. A lot of our computer hardware comes from Concorde, we don't want to see it slip under foreign control."

I look around the table. Stat and Snipe are in already. Blue nods his agreement to me. I look at Berk.

"What do you think?" he asks.

"I'm in," I say. I'm a marginalised minority, I'm a gay man with a husband and kid, I know what fake news does to the world.

"Me too then," Berk replies.

"Time to go to work, gentlemen. I'll let Edwards know." I stand up. "This is going to be light on equipment operation so Stat and Blue you are going to have to go in first, get us some local resources. Start coming up with a strategy. Berk, Snipe and I will follow on a couple of days after you, the less we are seen together the better."

Stat looks inquiringly at Blue and they both nod.

"Draft plans in six hours."

I can already feel the buzz in my blood, a mission, a cause, an adventure in the making. This is why I still work in the field. It still feels like we are somewhat on the side of the angels. Or if not the angels then at least not the devils.

Most of the time.

By our own screwy morality.

Ethan

I always struggle to sleep the first couple of nights Cameron is away. The bed feels huge without his big frame in it. I feel like a comet, lost in space, icy and cold, away from the gravity of him that drags me in.

He has always fascinated me, from the moment I met him. Which was totally the wrong time for me, for us, for a full blown relationship. I couldn't let him go though, even though I was in the midst of adopting Felix and making my work kid friendly.

Cameron, with his gentle smile and his sexy alter ego - damn, discovering that he was an animal between the sheets blew my mind! - his stoicism when I had to hurt him in therapy, his nerdy obsession with orchids. It was all just too irresistible.

We made it work though, and Felix got two Dads for the price of one dead Mama. I know it doesn't make up for what he's been through, but he has taken to this new family so well, maybe better than if it had been just me and him.

I roll over in bed and the faint traces of Cameron's body wash, musky and warm, tease me. I know it's sluttish but I didn't change the sheets after last night. I want his scent here a little longer.

This won't be a long trip, he promised, but his job is dangerous, one of the most dangerous in the world. He made that clear from the start, any trip could turn out to last forever.

I reach for my phone and check the time, it's just gone one in the morning. This night is going to be a slow one.

I wonder if it is dark where Cameron is. I wonder if he is diving already, if he is out there in the cold sunless depths of the sea, nothing between him and death but the ingenuity of man, and his ability to keep breathing in and out in times of extreme stress.

I don't think I could do it. I've watched films of it, of what he does, of the underwater drill heads, the ocean floor cables, and the massive pipelines. I've seen men like him, rough humanoid shapes in bulky dive gear moving slowly through the shadowy deep, dwarfed by all around them.

Cameron says the cold is what you remember most, it's always damn cold down there, but I think it's the vertigo that would get to me, not knowing which way is up in the darkness, all that depth above your head, ready to crush you.

With a sigh I sit up in bed. I'll never sleep now with all these images in my head. Once the imagination starts it just won't quit.

Quietly I pad in to check on Felix. He's in his usual sprawl on the bed, an untidy mess of limbs and thick red hair. He is snoring into his pillow, his face pressed into it. I move him onto his back so he can breathe easier, I don't want his sleeping position to trigger an asthma attack.

He snuffles and flails a little before settling onto his side, hands tucked beneath his chin.

I smile at him. He is so beautiful, the last living soul in the world with my blood. I would do anything for him. I spend a few minutes picking up things in his room, folding his clothes and quietly tidying his books away, an excuse to keep looking at him. He sleeps on, his eyeballs flickering under their thin lids as he dreams.

He doesn't have bad dreams so much anymore. He used to, when he first came to me, now he doesn't and I have to put a lot of that down to Cameron. He was always first at Felix's side when he woke up screaming, it was almost supernatural the speed with which he would wake up and be ready to act. I admit I leaned on it. I found it hard to deal with the terror on Felix's face, and then the disassociation, when his little face turned vacant and his eyes looked elsewhere. Cameron could always bring him back though, with his strong steady presence.

I make my way downstairs and put some ambient rain sounds on low on my phone and unroll my yoga mat in front of the dying fire. If I can relax enough I'll sleep here, if not I'll just meditate and try to stay in the moment until dawn. I've learned that's the only way to get through nights like these.

Settling onto the mat I perform a few stretches, trying to focus on my breath.

I think of Cameron in his tin can, breathing a mixture of gases that keep him alive at ridiculous depths. I don't know if the sat chamber is topside on the rig or down below for this job. Either way it will be cramped and uncomfortable and lack even basic privacy.

It's pretty selfish, sitting here, in our warm and safe living room, before the embers of an apple log fire, having had a shower, eaten a fresh cooked meal, and still feeling sorry for myself.

I acknowledge I am a poor human, and put the guilt aside.

I focus on my breathing, on my gratitude for this life, on my happiness that Felix is safe and well, and Cameron is a wonderful husband who will soon be home again.

Gradually I feel a sense of peace settle over me, and eventually my overactive brain slows.

Chapter Three

Camo

"Ready?" Snipe is a man of few words.

I nod and check my watch. We have four hours until our flight. Plenty of time.

"Blue and Stat have got a boat sorted, and Blue has sourced a couple of guns."

"I know. He could find arms in a convent." It never ceases to amaze me how Blue, who deals with most of the logistics, can sniff out illegal guns in any part of the world we go to.

"Shame I can't bring my rifle, it would be a quicker trip if I did."

"Yeah, but it would look very obvious. We're trying to make this one look like a robbery gone wrong."

Snipe shrugs, he thinks the obvious solution to any problem can be found through the sites of his high powered TAC-50.

If we were being dropped off by private jet or helicopter I'd be inclined to bring his sharp shooting skills to the front on this mission but we're going in through civilian means and a distant kill shot with the US navy seals favourite sniper rifle would be making it obvious who was behind this.

I slip a colourful aloha shirt over my dark wife beater and picking up a battered baseball cap I ram it on my head. Just a good ole boy going for some quality time in the Caribbean with his buds. It's a shallow role but a fun one.

I shoulder my bag and follow Snipe down the checkerboard metal stairs to the main floor of The Farm.

Edwards comes out of his office and nods at us. "Plan in shape?"

"Walk in the park." I can feel the sweet tension start to rise in me, running in ripples through my blood.

"Usual protocols for bug out and compromised." He tosses me a burner phone and I snatch it out of the air, the drip feed of adrenaline into my blood making me sharp.

I grin at him.

"Don't be cocky." It's been a few years since Edwards was in the field, maybe he doesn't remember how it makes you feel.

"Just ready to go."

Edwards nods, "I'll see you in a few days."

Berk is already behind the wheel of a nondescript silver hybrid. I climb into the passenger seat. Snipe takes the rear, leaning back and plugging in his headphones for the drive to the airport.

Berk, like me, is dressed in tourist casual, the only difference is he wears a long sleeved tshirt and fingerless gloves that cover the more obvious tattoos. He's still a pretty recognisable guy, with his full beard and height. He looks like door security on vacation though, not a martial arts specialist out to change the world, one asshole potential dictator at a time.

The drive to the airport is in silence. Snipe listens to music, Berk stares at the road and thinks his zen like thoughts, and my mind is with Blue and Stat already on location, building the foundations of the plan.

We leave the car in the short term car park. As we're idling in a queue waiting to enter departures Berk speaks up. "Where does your husband think you are?"

I look at him, surprised. "What makes you ask?"

"I might have met someone. I wondered how you managed it."

Berk is a bit more forthcoming than the other guys because we share a similar background. He has that military need to bond, but I've kept him at arm's length. I know he came out of a bad situation in the middle east, and the less said about that the better. I've seen the files, I've seen all their files, doesn't mean I talk to them about it.

"He thinks I'm two hundred foot down under the gulf," I say as I sling my bag onto the scanner belt.

"It's a good cover is it?"

"Works for me," I say, "I did a bit of it commercial diving after I got out so I know the score."

"Ever tempted to tell him?"

"Fuck, no!" I don't want this conversation. I never want Ethan to know. Ethan is gentle and good, he would never understand that there are reasons to kill. He doesn't need that in his life. Most people don't.

"Has he never suspected?" Jesus, I wish Berk would drop this.

"Nope, we're too busy being married."

Snipe pisses off and blends into the crowd, distancing himself from us.

"Does it bother you, lying to him?" Berk asks.

"Not much bothers me," I snap.

"Fair enough," he replies, finally taking the hint.

Within a couple of hours the multiple blues of the Caribbean sea are below. Berk is complaining there are no vegan options on the in flight menu and I look down at the sea and think about the lies I tell.

I chose my cover all those years ago because I love the sea. I did a stint as a commercial diver after I left the SEALs but it wasn't enough for me. The stress was too slow, a daily grind of relentless pressure rather than the sudden spikes I get in this role. And essentially it was grunt work in the dark. I spent a month up to my hips in sludge working on an exploratory drill rig and the only time I knew there was any life in the sea was when it bumped into me in the dark.

I watch the sea change from midnight blue to turquoise as we pass over an island of emerald green. The air is so clear I can see the curls of the currents as they carve around the island with its fringe of pale beaches.

Travel, sea, impending risk, this is the job for me.

Stat and Blue are waiting for us outside the terminal building on Guadeloupe. I take a deep breath of that dope heavy Caribbean air and ignore the calls of the porters as we weave through the crowds. Behind the palm trees that line the approach road there is a blood moon sinking out of view, it's going to be moonless for the next few nights. Always a good thing on these operations.

I slide into the passenger seat of the rental jeep and Berk and Snipe cram themselves into the back beside Blue. "Everything okay?" I ask.

"Yeah, got a decent boat, we can be on our way in a few hours, once the harbour quietens down."

The plan is to slip our moorings, run out without lights and make it across to Concord before morning. It's the busy season, there is a regatta about to take place on the island so we can lose ourselves amongst the flag waving hordes of yachties there to watch the big ships race. I doubt the infrequent patrol boats will even give a sideways glance once we are inside their territorial waters.

Early evening in the Caribbean smells of salt air and fish frying. The restaurants that line the marina are doing a roaring trade and Stat slows the jeep to move through the crowds of tourists and yacht crews that spill off the narrow sidewalks.

We pass docks bristling with high end sport fishing boats and rich man's toys with flying bridges and hot and cold running gold diggers. They have names like Bull Market and Paradise Acquired and home ports anywhere from Nassau to Valetta.

Climbing out of the jeep on the far side of the marina Stat indicates a boat tied up on the last pontoon. It's an old Parker Sport Cabin, 23ft long. Her dark green painted hull is scarred and faded but she rides high in the water. She's nondescript, the type of boat that is used everywhere around the Caribbean for snorkel tours and diving. The Parker is the workhorse of the tourist trade, totally innocuous, just what we need. She's got plenty of deck space and a tidy looking Yamaha outboard.

She's called Princess Putter. It could be worse.

I step onto the deck and it sways beneath my feet. Just that movement is enough to remind me that I love the sea, and how much I miss it. The evening breeze has risen, it brushes warm fingers along my skin. I can smell that unique scent of boats; engine oil, fish and adventure. I'm grinning as I drop my bag on the padded seat next to the centre console in the cabin.

"I checked the engine, she's got a four stroke 250 Yamaha. Blue and I stripped it, it's good, runs sweet." Stat says, "And she's got a Simrad system that's a lot newer than she is, it will get us there and back, piece of cake."

"She'll do," I say, surreptitiously patting the bulkhead because I'm a sap about old boats.

I spend the hours until cast off up on the bow, watching the lights of the marina and letting myself be lulled by the light slap of the waves against the hull. I've dropped into a kind of doze when Blue taps me on the shoulder just after 2am.

"Time to go," he says quietly.

Snipe slips the mooring ropes before jumping back on board and with Blue at the helm we slip out of the marina. In front of us the sea is inky blue, reflecting only gleams of starlight and behind us our wake is a thin curl of white edged with phosphorescence.

Steady and sure the small boat takes us across the channel towards Concorde, less than twenty nautical miles. The current is sluggish with only the run of the tide powering it and the lights of Guadeloupe quickly fade to pinpricks behind us. Once out of the lee of the island Blue opens up the Yamahas and Princess Putter points her nose in the air, kicks her ass a bit, and ploughs across the channel.

I keep my post at the bow, feeling the kiss of spray on my face. Just for a moment I wish Ethan was here, seeing this night and this sea and being part of the adventure. It's a crazy thought. I've never had it before. I wonder what brought it on now.

"What do you think?" I ask Blue.

We're parked up on a gravel pull in on a headland above a narrow strip of beach on the north end of Concorde. Across the channel the eastern half of Guadeloupe, Grande-Terre, is a low green mass on the horizon.

Blue has taken off his motorcycle helmet and is leaning casually on one of the pair of tired scooters we hired. At the far end of the beach below us steps rise up to a red roofed building amongst the palms and the jacaranda trees. I can see big white shuttered windows designed to catch the breezes and deep wrap around balconies.

"As expected," Blue replies, "There is a dock and steps up from the beach, one guard on the gate from the beach."

The candidate's home does not appear to be heavily fortified. The location is fairly remote on a promontory above a private beach - evil always wants to grab the best views - but we didn't see razor wire or any evidence of anything other than the most basic of electronic surveillance when we rode the scooters leisurely along the perimeter.

"Snipe and I could go in on our own," Blue says. I can see from the angle of his body and the way his torso sways, like a snake, that he wants that, a lot. "We don't need the whole team for this."

Snipe with a gun and Blue with a knife, it's a low risk play but I still feel uncomfortable letting my two known psychopaths out to play on their own. I know it's ridiculous but I still like to keep them where I can see them.

"No," I say, "Snipe stays on the boat with Stat. He hates swimming anyway. Berk and I will go in. You take out the gate guard and run rearguard."

Blue is mollified by the thought that he at least gets to hurt someone.

Down on the villa a tall thin man exits the house and stands on the balcony looking across at us. His body is all angles, long arms and legs with sharp joints, and his head juts forward on a thin neck making him look like an insect.

"Time to go," I say. Most people would look to the all encompassing sea view. "I think someone is interested in why we're so interested."

Keeping up the charade Blue takes one more look over the edge of the hillside at the beach below before he gets back on the scooter and pulls his helmet on.

"Reef on the right," he says, "Under the dock. Seagrass to the left until the last fifty foot when it's all sand, we'll stand out against it."

"Agreed," I reply, starting my engine. The little scooter whines before reluctantly starting. "We go in on the neighbouring bay. Stat will drop us offshore."

"Berk is going to moan about getting his beard wet."

"That's because he's a pussy." I say, and peel out onto the perimeter road that will take us back to the main harbour.

We drop the scooters at the backstreet shack we hired them from. The owner is already well on his way to blackout drunk from the cash we gave him. Then Blue and I make our way down the narrow streets towards the harbour.

Blue makes a detour to grab a load of patties from a laughing woman running a street food snack on a corner. She admonishes him when he buys twenty of the spicy half moon pastries dusted bright yellow with turmeric. "Yah got a helluva appetite there boy."

"You have no idea." He jogs back to me and just for a second he looks normal. A young man on a street bordered by brightly painted houses with tin roofs; tanned, blonde highlights in his hair, smiling, young and naturally hungry.

"The guys are going to love these," he says, "We couldn't stop eating them the last time we were here."

For all the blood and the gore and the losses Blue had more chances than most at a normal life. His brother and brother in law are about as high as it gets in the Handler system. Thanks to them he got to travel, he got freedoms that Snipe would have given his right eye for.

A shadow crosses his face as he realises what he has said, and normal vanishes.

I take the bag of patties from him. "Good thinking," I say, "Nothing like a full stomach to give the team morale."

I have never had an operation go so badly wrong.

From the word go it's a shit show.

The plan was the boat would drop Berk, Blue and I off a couple of hundred yards off shore, we'd swim into the beach adjacent to Brown's seaside compound. We'd take the gate guard, Blue would hold it while Berk and I would go in and fake a robbery with deadly side effects. We'd be back on the beach in short order and swim back out to the boat. We'd be back on Guadeloupe for breakfast, home by dinner time.

On paper it looked sweet.

The weather was the first thing that didn't help.

A Norte came up, a cold and biting wind that in the Caribbean closes harbours and sends tourists shivering. August Brown's compound was in the lee of the wind being on the north west coast but the sea was still lumpy, the visibility was shit, and when we got in the water the current was a bitch.

It takes us twice as long as I expected to swim to shore and Berk, despite his fitness, is breathing hard when we pull ourselves out onto the rocky shore.

Driving rain is plastering Blue's hair to face. "Is Stat going to see our return signal in this?"

"Should do," I say, "I told him to stay in closer, but let's get this done. At least the wind and rain will hide his engine noise."

"Knew I should have brought the night scope," Blue frets.

Berk rises slowly to his feet. "More cardio for you," I say with a push to his shoulder, trying to raise a smile. "That swim took it out of you."

"In your dreams," he grunts back.

Blue leads the way over the rocks of the headland, Berk and I hang back and get our guns out. We watch as he slips back into the water under the dock, using it as cover. He climbs up inside the scaffolding like steps to where, through the rain, I can see a guard in a waterproof green poncho pressed back against the gate trying to get some shelter.

Blue is a shadow with steel in his hand as he silently climbs onto the platform. One second the guard is standing, the next he is slumping against Blue.

As Berk and I climb the stairs from the beach I hear the dull thump of something heavy hitting the sand below us. When we get to the gate Blue is wearing the green poncho, hood up over his head, and there is no sign of a body.

"Good call," I say briefly.

That's the last good thing that happens.

"Hold the gate," says Berk with a smirk as he and I enter the grounds.

"Oh, ha de ha ha," Blue snarls, edgy and clearly wanting more blood.

There are a few lights still glowing in the very top windows of the villa when Berk and I approach through the gardens, but they are turned low, just accent lighting. All exterior lights are off, and we can't hear or see any patrolling guards.

Fucking ridiculous, I think to myself, lousy security.

We could go in under the house, it's built on stilts to make the most of the view and protect against flash floods, but I change my mind when we get there. There are steps to the side that weren't obvious in the satellite photos. Dense greenery backs them and they are deep with shadows. The fronds of juvenile palms wave wildly in the wind, they will cover our movements.

I motion for Berk to go that way. He takes point up the steps and we silently glide onto the balcony. Heavy tarpaulin covers have been rolled down over the balcony and they sway in the wind, rattling softly when they hit the railings.

Berk tries the handle of a screen door, it slides open silently. I take up the point position, automatic up and safety off, and he follows me in, closing the door behind and taking position behind my left shoulder.

This is the second floor. There is one floor below us, mainly storage apparently, and two and half floors above us. This level has the kitchen and living areas, the main suite is the next floor up, staff in the attic rooms.

Passing out of the living room I note the door to the kitchen and a corridor leading towards the stairs. Low level lights illuminate the dark wood floors and I move confidently down the corridor, my automatic at the ready, glancing back now and then to check behind.

We turn a corner and find the stairs. One flight up, one flight down.

"Take the role," I whisper to Berk, "I'll stay here."

He nods and starts up the stairs, his steps silent in his rubber boots, his gun at the ready.

According to schematics the main suite is directly in front of the stairs. All Berk has to do is go in, shoot the guy, throw some stuff around and leave.

The house is silent around me. It's almost like I can hear it breathing, expectant.

I glance at my wrist computer, two minutes. Any second now. I wait for the muffled sound of a gunshot.

I breathe quietly, any second now.

I should have done this myself.

Without warning lights start flashing in the corridor and my ears are assaulted by blaring sirens. I actually duck, expecting to feel bullets impact on my body. Faintly above the wail of sirens I hear the pop of a gunshot.

I look up, Berk is barreling down the stairs. His face above the black beard is bone white.

I don't ask questions, we don't have time. I turn and race down the corridor, assuming Berk is behind me.

As I reach the living room I can hear shouting behind me.

I don't look back, sliding open the balcony door and making the stairs down to the grounds in a few seconds.

By the time I'm at the gate the whole house is blazing with lights and the sirens are still blaring.

"What the fuck happened? Where's Berk?" Blue's restlessness is obvious, he moves from one foot to the other, his right hand spinning his blade on his palm.

I look behind me, there is no Berk.

"Shit, stay here, I'll go back."

"Let me go," Blue's voice is urgent, "They might have seen you, I'm something else, it gives me an advantage."

"No, I know the layout better, stay here, signal Stat, we're going to be coming in hot."

The adrenaline is fizzing in my blood and even though Berk is in trouble I still love the feeling. It gives me energy and I sprint back up the grounds.

Confused men in fatigues are milling underneath the stilts of the house. There are at least ten of them, their torch beams stabbing the dark beneath the pilings. The basement floor must be a damn barracks. I stick to the side path, deep in the shadows. The door to the second level is still wide open.

Cautiously I peer inside. Flashing lights, screaming sirens, and above that I can hear yelling. Keeping to the edges of the room I creep to the door to the corridor.

The corridor is a mess of people. Guards and staff and someone is screaming hysterically. In the midst of it is Berk. He's like a wild animal at bay, his teeth bared, tugging at his hair. He hasn't got a gun in his hands but he has a lot pointed at him.

"Na la akil lahm albaqar 'aw aldaan 'aw aldajaji! la taqtuluu alhayawanati! alhayawanat laha 'arwahun!" Berk is yelling angrily, and the men with guns pointed at him don't know what to make of it.

The only foreign language Berk speaks is bad arabic, and with his thick black beard and eyes there is a chance, in the dark, on a rainy night, he could be taken for one. I'm pretty sure he is telling them he is vegan though so hopefully nobody understands him.

One guard takes the initiative, or just gets nervous and fires. Berk jerks and howls in rage as the bullet goes through his bicep and into the wall behind him.

"'Ant abn alkhanzir" Berk slaps a hand over the wound in his arm, drops his head and rushes the guards.

It's the last thing they expect and I get a split second to open fire before he barrels into them. With a maniac in front and gunfire from behind they do the right thing and panic. I maybe hit one or two but it's an accident, I'm aiming high, I don't want to hit Berk. Most drop to the floor and take cover - conscripts, no backbone.

I grab Berk's good arm to steady him as he flounders over bodies. We call him Berk for a reason, it's short for Berserk, and the red mist has clearly descended.

"Run," I growl at him, and he takes off down the corridor.

I turn my back on the guards and race after him. The sirens are still blaring, the flashing lights are blinding. Berk is gone and I sure as hell hope he remembered the way out in the midst of his rage.

I need to cover our tracks as much as possible. This house is not as defenceless as we imagined. With panic alarms, sirens and lights as well as a cadre of guards in the basement I would be stupid to think they didn't have electronic surveillance too, and I walked through the place like I owned it.

There is an exit through the kitchen. I swerve off the most direct route out and head for it. Lots of things in a kitchen can damage a house.

Even here there are flashing lights and sirens. Overkill I feel. I pause, scanning the room before rapidly turning on all the burners on the stove. There is a huge bin of flour on the worktop. I heave it over to a central prep table and knock it over, spilling the flour out.

Might work. Should work.

I throw open the kitchen door and the Norte comes streaming in. I dash through the door. Glancing back I see the flour rising in a cloud from the prep table. It drifts, eddying in the air, filling the room with tiny particles. Flammable particles in fire fueling air.

I keep running.

Behind me there is silence and then a loud explosion as the burners ignite the flour and the windows blow out. I look back and see flames leaping behind shattered glass.

"What the fuck did you do?" Berk gasps when I reach him and Blue at the gate.

"Flour bomb," I say, "Now go."

Blue is frantically waving a torch. "He can't see us."

"Get to the end of the dock."

We fly down the steps to the beach, taking them two and three at a time.

Berk seems to be holding up well despite the arm wound. His mouth is a thin line and his eyes are wild but I think he has control of himself.

At the end of the dock the waves are breaking over the pilings, dark grey and angry looking.

Blue waves the flashlight again and I glance back at the compound building, it's burning well but there are lights coming down the path through the grounds.

"Come on, Stat, bring her in." Berk growls.

Above the sound of the wind and the waves I can hear the dull throb of an engine. Through the rain I see a dull glimmer of red. Red for port. Stat has the boat pointed nose into the Norte. I take a bearing with my wrist compass. "Two fifty degrees, swim straight ahead the current will take us down to him." I bark, "Get in the water."

Hold her steady, Stat, I think to myself as I slide off the end of the dock and a wave slaps me in the face. Just keep her there.

He's only seventy five yards off shore, taking a helluva risk on the rocks. I can hear the engine thrumming and the sound of the waves on her hull as she hurdles the swells the Norte is sending around the tip of the island.

I hang back, making sure Blue and particularly Berk make it.

Stat, bless his thorough little heart, has thrown out a buoy and when Berk is swept past the stern by the current he manages to grab it.

Blue, already onboard, is assisted by Snipe in heaving Berk out of the water.

This feels like fucking basic training all over again as I hang onto the side of the boat, waiting my turn, face covered in snot and head spinning mildly as I ride the swells, kicking on the rise to keep my head out of the water.

I clamber on board without assistance, resting on my hands and knees on the deck. I can see Stat turn towards me by the glow of the instrument panel.

"Douse the running lights, get us the fuck out of here," I say.

Stat spins the wheel and Princess Putter wallows wildly in the swell, turning away from the shore and out across the channel.

Wearily I haul myself to my feet and into the cabin. "That was a fucking disaster. The place was wired up all to hell. If we got out of that without being caught on camera it will be the second luckiest day of my life."

"Shall I call a compromised code?"

"No, not yet, let's get across to Guadeloupe and then assess."

I brace myself against the swells in the cabin doorway. Snipe is dealing with Berk's arm wound. He's stripped off his wetsuit and rash vest and has the first aid kit open at his feet. Blue is hunkered down in the shelter of the cabin wall. His face is as calm as ever, he looks like he is taking part in a yacht race off the Hamptons.

The rain is tailing off but the wind is blowing just as strongly and the first aid kit is sliding across the wet deck.

"What the hell went wrong?" I ask Berk.

He looks up at me, his face haunted. "There was a dead kid in the room. Just lying there on the bed. I froze. The target came out of the bathroom, saw me, hit a panic button before I could shoot him."

"Why weren't you behind me when we ran?"

"I had to throw up, and then I lost it."

Behind us I can see the glow of the fire still burning in the Brown villa and every light is on in the grounds. I can see powerful searchlights scanning the grounds and the sea in front.

Thank fuck we got out before someone made it up to them, we would have been sitting ducks.

A particularly big swell causes the boat to toss her nose in the air before smashing down and wallowing in the trough. I see Berk grit his teeth, his arm held tight across his side.

"We got a problem," Snipe calls to me. He points to the south. His excellent vision has spotted lights coming up from the main harbour on Concorde. With the port closed to normal traffic due to the Norte that can only be a patrol boat.

Of course they are going to focus the search at sea, we went in wearing fucking wetsuits.

They can't be sure where we are but they are faster than us, they have searchlights and they are armed to the teeth - when you haven't got much of a standing army military types like to spend money on boats and planes.

Fuck.

Time for a Plan B.

Did I make a Plan B?

"How far to Guadeloupe territorial waters?" I ask Stat.

He glances at the Simrad. "About seven nautical miles and I'm getting maybe 20mph out of her at the moment, this sea is heavy."

Under half an hour then, give or take, to the invisible border but I doubt these guys are going to pay much attention to that if they have us in their sights.

So, seven nautical miles to the border, another ten to land, more if we want to land somewhere convenient. That's going to be well over an hour but Stat can open her up once the Norte lets up in the lee of Guadeloupe.

"What's their heading?" I call back to Snipe.

He stares through the darkness, watching for the lights above the dip and rise of the waves.

"Bad news, they've turned into the channel, they assume we're making a straight run for it."

And they would be right.

We watch as the lights behind us grow closer and soon we can make out the beam of searchlight, scanning the water, sweeping in wide arcs, turning the black sea murky grey.

"We've crossed the border," Stat mutters, "We're in Guadeloupe waters now."

"Not stopping them," says Snipe.

Shit.

I take a deep breath. "We need to get as close to the Guadeloupe shore as possible," I say, "And then we're going to swim for it."

"I hate swimming," says Berk sourly.

"Me too," agrees Snipe.

Blue just slides into the cabin and takes over the wheel from Stat who starts checking his dry bag.

As we pass the eastern point of Guadeloupe and the ragged pinnacles of Pointe De Chateau the wind drops, the sea smoothes out, and Blue opens the engine another few notches.

We're not going to make it anywhere convenient though, they are too close behind us now and if they have radioed Guadeloupe for assistance we could be caught between a rock and a hard place.

"Turn us north again," I say looking back at the sweeping searchlights. "There's a beach on the other side of the point. If we can get upwind of it the current will take us in."

"I know the one you mean."

I don't ask how.

Stat has pulled on a wetsuit, he has a dry bag slung over his chest. Our paperwork, our money, our way out will be in there along with the phone. I debate calling a compromised code now, but it might be picked up.

"What are you going to do with the boat?" he asks.

"Deep six."

"Shit, I liked this boat."

"So did I."

Snipe is helping Berk do up his wetsuit. Berk doesn't like swimming but Snipe really hates water. He's like a cat, he likes to be dry and warm, because of the childhood that never was.

Blue drives us head on through the waves, getting us north of the jagged rocks of the island's tip. When I think we're far enough north and close enough in I send the team into the water. Blue hands me the helm. "See you onshore." He's gone, over the side with a run and a jump.

I set the autopilot and open up the valve on the small gas canister we have in the cabin. It's there to power the little stove we've been cooking on. It's at least half full.

I hear the hiss of the gas as I shut the cabin door, letting the small space fill with propane.

I slice the line on the auxiliary fuel tank and the rush of fumes makes my eyes water.

I step onto the starboard running deck and move forward to the bow. I won't have much time once I get in the water.

I step off into the blackness.

The water closes over my head and I twist towards where the boat was, watching the bubbles, silver in the darkness, showing me the way up. I break the surface easily, letting a rolling swell lift me. Blinking water out of my eyes I look for the boat and raise my arm. I held tight to my automatic as I entered the water, cradling it against my chest. I didn't want to drop it.

The boat is already a good twenty yards away. I slide into the trough of a wave and the boat disappears. As I rise on the next crest she sways into sight, already wallowing as the autopilot sends her ploughing on mindlessly.

I fire as she comes into view, pumping shot after shot at her cabin as the wave takes me up.

A shot goes through the side window of the cabin. The gas filled interior ignites in a ball of flame. My second fire of the night.

I let the gun drop from my hand, barreling down in the deep, and turn towards the shore, letting the waves take me, and the current help me along. It's less a swim, more a ride, just stay afloat and let mother nature send you home.

I'm still exhausted when I pull myself out onto the powder white sand of the crescent beach below the headland of Pointe des Chateaux. Dawn is coming, there is a faint glow to the horizon in front of me. In a few minutes I'll be able to see the cross at the top of the headland.

I make a mental note to say thanks when I do. Right now though I need to get off the beach.

And I am going to have to suck up my pride, chow down on humble pie, and call in a compromised code for the first time ever.

Chapter Four

Ethan

A news channel, one of the less editorially suspect ones, is playing on the waiting room wall screen as I collect my last patient of the day. I glance at it as I cross the room to help Mrs Montgomery, who recently had a double hip replacement, out of her chair. On the screen grainy black and white footage is showing a man walking down a corridor with a gun in his hand. Something about it draws my eye.

I see the word Concorde underneath the film, part of a trailing news headline.

"Look at me, Dr Ethan, I'm ready to go back to tea dances." I pull my eyes away from the screen and back to my patient. Mrs Montgomery is out of her chair and gives me a twirl - double hip replacements, better than a cup of water from the fountain of youth.

I smile widely at her. "You'll have to teach me to dance so I can come with you."

Something nags at me. Something familiar.

It's still bothering me when I say goodbye to Mrs Montgomery. It's like I have missed something.

I glance at my watch, I have an hour for admin before I have to leave to relieve the babysitter.

I check my phone as I wait for my laptop to boot up, just in case Cameron has had a chance to send a text. I don't check during work time, sometimes his messages can be a bit risque and blushes tend to linger with my colouring.

There is nothing from Cameron and I turn to the laptop, pulling up my online records database. Just before the page loads I catch a glimpse of that grainy film again in the headlines. Something nags at me.

I remember Cameron walking into the bedroom the other night. He has this way about him when he is feeling sexy and dominant. A certain swagger, a certain 'alphaness'. It's when the relaxed and easy going man I married goes away and a more primal part of his personality comes out to play. His whole body changes.

I spend my life studying bodies, how they move, how they present, how they work. I know instantly when Cameron is feeling his testosterone levels, it shows in every line of him. He seems taller, his hips roll more as he moves, the angle of his head changes and his shoulders straighten. He goes from guy next door to predator in the blink of an eye.

I find it sexy as hell. It makes me want to get on my knees for him and do anything he asks.

From the very first time he took me to bed I saw that part of him. Once the suit came off the man below was revealed and he was amazing. Muscle and sexual intent. Big hands and a cock I wanted to worship. It's like in owning his own body he owns mine. He blew my mind.

What makes me think of that now?

I close the data sheet and click onto the news headlines.

It's a slow news day; President greets sportsmen at White House, some celebrity has done something sexy online and people are divided about it, there has been an assassination in the Caribbean.

I click the Caribbean headline and a news report plays.

"The Caribbean island of Concorde has been rocked today by the assassination of the main opposition candidate, August Brown, in the upcoming presidential elections."

The bland host is replaced by a picture of a paradise island in a turquoise sea. There is a montage of beaches, marches involving the election, and drone shots of an expansive factory in a vivid green landscape.

"Concorde, a country which has enjoyed unparalleled economic growth in recent years under the guidance of sitting President Andrews, is in turmoil after footage was released showing apparent foreign mercenaries in the home of Mr Brown shortly before the shooting."

The grainy footage is playing. An almost featureless corridor, a man dressed in tight fitting black is walking down it with a gun at arm's length, a shadow behind and to the side showing he isn't alone. He turns his head to look behind him at the way he has come and then moves out of the camera view.

"One man was briefly captured but then escaped. He was described as heavily bearded and possibly arabic.

"President Andrews has condemned the assassination and has publically vowed that if international parties are responsible for this act of treason they will be brought to justice."

There is a still shot from the footage. A close up of the man's head. No features are discernable in the footage, it's the standard blurry security footage. Who has security cameras inside their home?

"Mr Brown was apparently shot at close range and his body was discovered by his security personnel as they attempted to remove him from the property which was on fire at the time."

More video, drone footage of a headland under pearly grey skies, a smoke stained house overlooking a beach.

"In other news, the Suez Canal..."

I put the video back to its starting point and watch it again.

Then I watch it with the sound off.

Then I go looking for longer versions.

Inside the nagging feeling isn't nagging anymore. It's feeling sort of sick.

I shut my laptop down and go home.

Mindlessly I cook supper and get Felix into bed. I think I read to him. I must read to him, I always do.

I go to the bedroom and open the closet doors. I look at Cameron's clothes, his suits he hardly ever wears, his folded tees on the shelves, his array of boots on the floor on his side.

His current favourite orchid is on the bedside table. A white oncidium hybrid with dark brown spots, it smells delicious, almost like baby powder and it's nodding flowers dance as I walk past it.

Somewhere in my head the footage keeps playing.

If someone wasn't who they said they were, how would you know?

I fish my phone out of my pocket and scroll through my contacts.

If someone lived a secret life how could you tell?

You could follow them - unless you lived on land and they worked at sea.

You could call their company - unless they are freelance.

You could ask their friends and colleagues - I have only ever met Stat, and I don't even know his full name.

Sometimes it's not the evidence, it's the lack of evidence.

In my head Cameron again walks into the bedroom, he glances behind him to check the door is shut. That movement, that turn of the head, checking behind, it was so smooth, so automatic.

If you are a predator you need to be aware.

That's what Cameron is. He's aware. All the time. Even when he is lazy and laid back and chilling out. I have never made him jump, never surprised him with my presence. He knows where he is at all times.

Maybe that's a diver thing? You need good spatial awareness, you always need to know which way is up.

My head aches.

I force myself to take a shower, eat some food and climb into bed. I sleep, but I dream of Cameron, dressed all in black, stalking towards me with a gun in his hand.

When I wake, at dawn, there is a text on my phone from Cameron.

'Should be home in 36hrs, only another few hours until decompression is over. Sick of the way these guys squeak at me, can't wait to make you moan!"

I shut myself in the bathroom. I feel as though my world is shuddering around me, the pillars of my life dissolving like ghosts. I know my husband when I see him. I can't deny that.

I saw my husband on that footage. I would know him anywhere.

It takes a long time for the anger to come and when it does it is a cold thing at first, spreading throughout my limbs like a hard frost.

Camo

We spend a day holed up in a hot hotel room before Janus can get us out. He gets Stat and Berk on a flight to Atlanta and then on to Washington. Blue goes it solo, hopping to Fort Lauderdale and then up the coast, he will be back at the farm first.

I get stuck with Snipe. I suppose that is better than being with Berk who has been made to shave his beard off. It knocks a decade off his appearance but he isn't happy about it.

Snipe and I island hop on the ferry over to St Lucia and then get a flight onto New York and shuttle to DC.

I spend the time between dragging myself onto the beach and dragging myself off the plane in Washington DC kicking myself.

Stat, reliable as ever, is waiting for us landside. He's got an extra half inch of stubble on his cheeks and black half circles under his blue eyes. Berk must have whined like a baby.

There are protocols in place within military organisations to deal with mission failure, to deal with fuck ups and poor prep and poor teamwork. There are chains of command, questions get asked, mistakes get accounted for, and training corrects against it happening again (hopefully).

We don't have that.

We're too young an organisation with too neurodivergent a team.

We have to thrash it out ourselves. Any which way that works.

And we will.

Just not tonight.

It's too soon for a debrief, too soon for finger pointing, too soon for anything other than to sit quietly, lick our wounds, hate ourselves, and know we got out by the skin of our teeth.

Edwards is there to greet us at The Farm. Well, greet is probably too friendly a word. He's there. And he's unhappy and I can totally understand why.

He doesn't say anything, he doesn't need to, he just shakes his head at me and his one remaining eye seems to glitter like a terminator on reserve batteries.

I shrug and don't say anything. I just want to get home now. I've had enough of acting for a while. I want to be myself and go kiss my husband and wind up my kid.

I know this is all on me. I made bad decisions and I didn't take advantage of my team's skills. I was in a rush to get in and get out on a mission I thought was a walk in the park.

I should have had Stat run a full surveillance before we finalised the plan, first and foremost that was the biggest mistake. We were woefully unprepared for the kind of electronic surveillance that was in the compound.

Even after that there were a hundred things I could have done differently.

I should have brought Blue with me into the compound, he would not have been caught, he would have taken out Brown before he had a chance to hit the panic button.

I should have had Snipe stationed shoreside with a sniper rifle as back up, even if it took a while to source one.

On the ground I made every decision and I made them with a hot head, spur of the moment. That's not always a bad thing but in this instance it was stupid.

We should have rescheduled when the Norte started. We could have run anywhere other than straight for Guadeloupe after we got out. We could have ditched the boat and gone landside.

I swear, once I get some sleep I am going to come back here and we're going to go over this and I'm going to admit my mistakes. We were matched as a team because our psychological profiles make up for each other's shortcomings. I'm not giving my guys a chance to show their skills. That has to change. Leading from the front is a good way, but it's not the only way.

The debrief on this role will be a doozy.

"Can you drop me home?" I ask Stat. He's tired himself, he only got in a couple of hours ago but he nods and we make a sharp exit. Edwards doesn't try to stop us. The others will do whatever their thing is that they do to get back in the right mindset and we'll go over all this later.

At least none of us are dead.

At least the role was carried out.

At least we didn't get caught.

I'm pretty sure if I was still in the military we would be calling that a win. At least in public.

Here it just shows up the cracks in our system, we never really ironed the kinks out. We made it back from this by the skin of our teeth and we all know it. Lessons will be learned. But later, not right now.

Ethan

I hear his key in the door and I wait, hugging my knees, sitting quietly.

The door opens and he comes in, dropping his kit bag on the wooden floor just inside the entrance and sighing tiredly.

The room is dim and he hasn't seen me. I can tell from his posture that he is exhausted. There is a tension across his shoulders that wasn't there when he left me.

He scrubs his hands over his short hair and looks around, wondering why nobody has greeted him.

He sees me huddled in the oversize armchair beside the unlit fireplace.

We just stare at each other.

One thing about married couples, no matter how much they lie to each other when they choose to show the truth, the other one can read it clearly.

It takes effort to lie in a marriage, the closeness becomes automatic over time. That is one of the myriad of things that have been churning in my head since I worked this out. Cameron made the effort to do this, and it worked.

"What is it?" His voice is low and gruff, I can hear long roads and old adrenaline in it.

"In case you are concerned it isn't Felix."

He might think fuck all of me but he loves Felix, of that I am sure, and that will be where his mind goes first.

"Is something wrong with you?"

"More you."

"Can it wait, babe, it's been a helluva few days. We nearly lost Berk."

"I know."

He steps closer, the light of the lamp on the side table casts a glow across his face. His scruff is thicker than when he left, he is squinting with tiredness, his mouth is set in a grim line.

For a moment I feel a flutter of anxiety, if Cameron is the man on the tv then he is a killer.

"How do you know about Berk?"

"It was on the tv."

Various expressions flash across his face - I see worry morph into calculation and then settle into resignation.

He doesn't bother denying it.

I did hope he would. I have never wanted to be wrong more in my life. If he was good enough he might even have been able to persuade me I was mistaken.

It seems I am not worth the effort.

Slowly he sinks down into the couch across from me, distractedly he pulls one of Felix's comic books from under his thigh and drops it on the floor. He rubs his hands over his face and then his shoulders straighten. "I don't know where to start," he says, and he shrugs like this is all so much weight on his shoulders.

It's the shrug that makes me mad. Like he's the one that has to organise this, sort it out, pick a place to start. Must be a real effort for him.

"How long?" My voice is a hiss I don't recognise.

"How long, what?" He looks confused. "How long have I been doing what I do, or how long have I been lying to you?"

I feel as though I am slowly coming to the boil, the normally calm surface of my mind disturbed by hot currents, miniscule bubbles rising, anger growing. I push it down. Not yet.

"Take your pick."

"When I met you I was part of the Handler system, I was support staff. I have been lying to you since the day I met you." His voice is even, no inflection, no shame, no excuses.

"So you hadn't hurt your shoulder in a diving accident when I met you?"

"It was a bullet wound, I got caught in the crossfire helping a Handler with a gang situation. The bullet got lucky and got past my kevlar."

"The Handler system doesn't exist any more."

"No. For the last two years I have been a member of another organisation, we work on an international basis undertaking critical and sensitive missions."

"Why the lies?" I don't know how I am staying so calm.

"Nobody needs to know."

"I'm not nobody."

"No." he says, "You're my husband, I love you, and you didn't need to know."

That's when I lose my temper.

I surge to my feet, I want to hit him. I won't let myself hit him because I might never stop.

"You're a fucking killer," I scream at him, "You were on the news. You assassinated a foreign politician."

The impact of what I am saying hits me. I never thought my life would be like this, my marriage would be like this. I find myself swaying backwards and sagging into the armchair.

Cameron is silent.

Between us the blonde wood floors stretch like a desert.

"It's a secret." He almost whispers it. "What we do is secret. You aren't meant to know, it's better like that."

"Not for me," I say wearily, "How can you have let me make the choices I made when I didn't know this."

"Because I wanted the things you chose. I wanted you, I wanted a family, I wanted it all."

"It's not fair."

"I know." I feel his exhaustion. I would swap it for my own. All I want to do is have him go away and then I can sleep. Find oblivion. Not have to think about this anymore.

I wasn't wrong. My husband is a killer. And I don't know what that does to our future.

"You need to leave."

He doesn't question me, just gets up and walks towards the door.

"Felix?" he asks.

"At a friend's house."

"Okay, that's good." He lifts his car keys from the bowl on the table beside the door and wearily picks up his kit bag. I don't know if I expected more of an argument, or at least some remorse, or an explanation.

It's probably best he doesn't try and explain, I don't know if I could take it in right now. I just feel like I am falling, like the ground I stood on has been washed from under my feet.

Once I get my head above water that's when we can talk, then I can find out how deep the lies run.

There is a quiet click as Cameron closes the door behind him and I realise I know nothing about him. I don't know where he will go or what he will do. I don't know how much of our lives was real, or if our only truth was the feel of our bodies together.

Chapter Five

Camo

Stat hands me a coffee and doesn't ask questions. He answered the gate monitor at The Farm last night and when I said I was staying for a while he said nothing. He was at his computer array when I walked into the main room.

"Which room is spare?"

He glanced at me, taking in the exhaustion, assessing my state of mind. "Top of the stairs, straight ahead. Towels in the closet."

"Thanks."

I went upstairs, dropped my bag, showered, crawled into bed and slept like the dead.

Don't think about it.

Now, sitting at the industrial metal table in the kitchen I just want to drink coffee and be left alone.

Edwards slides onto the bench seat opposite me. He's wearing black combat pants and a tight long sleeve t-shirt. He must be here to work out with one of the boys or he would be in a suit. I'd hoped to avoid him while I worked out what the fuck was going on.

"Got something to tell me?" he asks.

"Ethan knows."

"The security camera footage?"

By the time I called in the compromised code from the beach on Guadeloupe Edwards had already known about the security camera footage. He was suitably abrupt and said he had Janus on it.

"Ethan recognised me on the fucking news. It must have been a slow news day, they ran the security camera footage on me over the story of the assassination."

"It didn't show your face."

"He's my fucking husband, he recognised me." I wearily rub my eyes.

"And?"

"And, he kicked me out, he's insane with fury."

Berk walks into the room, sees Edwards and I and turns on his heel and walks out again.

Go team!

Fuck, I have put all these guys in jeopardy with this. I have fucked up my marriage. I am a god damn disaster.

Edwards huffs out a breath. I look up at him. I don't think this is the kind of situation he has much experience with because he looks uncomfortable.

"You don't need to say anything," I tell him, "This is all on me."

"Obviously."

"I'll sort it out."

"If you need help..."

"You'll do what?"

"I have no idea, but I think that is what people say in circumstances like this isn't it?"

"Not in this world."

The silence grows between us.

Edwards knocks on the table, it's the most awkward I have ever seen him. "I'm going to spar with Berk, then I'll be in my office if you want to talk."

I can't imagine how that would help.

"Can we just pretend this isn't happening?" I say.

He nods with relief, "Sure, we can do that while you figure it out."

Under my fists the punchbag feels like a bag of cement. I put my shoulder behind the punches and all it does is hurt. Everything hurts, and achieves nothing.

Sweating and frustrated I grab the bag, hugging it.

"Berk," I call out to the massive ex-marine, "Come spar with me, I need something real."

"Not today, Camo, I've already gone some with Edwards and my bicep isn't healed."

"Pussy," I taunt him.

"I can hurt you if you like," Blue offers, "If you want to feel something."

"I'll pass, I'm pissed with myself, I don't have a deathwish."

"Who is the pussy now?" Blue arches an eyebrow at me.

I'm thinking about resigning. I'm thinking about quitting. Going home to Ethan and laying it all out for him to judge. If Ethan will take me back I'll shut it all down. But if I have a choice, if he gives me a choice, I want to make it up to my team first.

These aren't bad men and they have chosen to do something dangerous for good reasons. I have let them down, leading them the wrong way. Shit, I'm forty one now, I should have got the hang of it.

I rest my sweating forehead against the course weave of the punchbag.

When did I fall into the pattern of thinking I was the only one with the right ideas?

I think it's because I had Ethan. Ethan's love and his acceptance of me made me think I was bulletproof, always right. Which clearly I am not. I'm just a really good liar at the end of the day, and being good at that isn't enough.

Ethan

"When is Dad coming home?" Felix's dark head is bent over his sketchbook as I make dinner for two. "He sent me a text yesterday saying he would be home last night."

Shit, I forgot that Cameron often did that.

I have a rule with Felix - I don't lie to him. No matter how hard the topic or how much of a struggle it is I try to put it in a way he can understand. It has always been that way with us. From the day I picked him up from Child Services after his mother overdosed.

He had been trapped in the apartment with his dead mother for two days and the moment I saw him, with his distant eyes and his down turned mouth I knew that already this kid had been let down and lied to a lot. I wasn't going to be another adult who did that to him.

I guess that's why I am so broken-hearted about Cameron. My sister was a habitual liar although on the good days I try to think of it as wishful thinking. The thought that my husband is the same makes me think this is all just history repeating.

"You Dad won't be home today," I say, "He and I have had a disagreement."

Felix's head jerks up and that wary look I hate is back in his eyes. Never have I been more tempted to be economical with the truth.

"Is he not going to live here anymore?"

"I don't know. It was a bad disagreement. I think it will take a while to sort out, but you will still be seeing him."

Cameron will keep seeing Felix if I have to staple the boy to his big broad chest.

"Are you getting a divorce?"

Is it right that every kid over the age of four knows what divorce is?

"Divorce is not something that has been mentioned at all."

"I don't want you to get a divorce." He whispers it as though he dare not express the desire. I can see him sinking back into himself like he first did when he came to me, drawing away, going to the deep place inside where he feels he can't be seen.

"I don't want a divorce either, small child." I tell him and I find I mean it. "I want to sort it out because that is what good people do, they try and sort out their problems."

I reach out and take his hand. It lies passively in my grasp.

"Don't worry Felix, it will all be okay, that I can promise you."

I don't know if he can hear me, he sits like a small solemn statue. This is how he is when he is upset or confused, or when something he didn't see coming has happened. He isn't good with shock, my damaged little boy.

I move around the counter and wrap my arms around him from behind. He is warm and smells so familiar and I don't know if I am giving comfort or getting it. I press a kiss to his hair.

"Everything is okay, Felix," I tell him firmly, "Everything will be fine. You are loved. You are safe. You are not alone."

He shivers a little, and I feel him come back to me. Touch helps. Cameron was always so good at giving him that. The security of a hug in big strong arms.

"How about you send your Dad a message now, ask him if it is okay to call him."

I know Cameron will want to speak to Felix and I know he will say the right thing. We were always on the same page with Felix.

Now I wonder if that was because he had a lot more experience dealing with the damaged than I had previously thought.

It wasn't long after Felix came to me that I met Cameron. Felix and I were a package deal from the start and Cameron was always so good with him. Endlessly patient, getting up with him and holding him when he had nightmares, making sure to keep in touch while he was away, doing everything possible to bring him out of his shell.

I don't think that was an act.

I'm so confused, I don't know what was real and what wasn't anymore. But I am sure that Cameron will always be there for Felix.

Felix's small fingers are flying over his phone screen, he records a quick video message and sends it. The kid is barely six and he is better with tech than either Cameron or I. I move back around the counter and carry on with dinner.

Cameron's reply, thankfully, comes quickly, Felix's phone making the bubbling sound that is Cameron's signature ringtone - that pisses me off, he wasn't blowing bubbles, he was blowing smoke up my ass.

Felix answers the video call, his face serious and his listening look in place.

I hear Cameron's voice on the video, his voice is tinny through the speakers and I strain to hear him. I want to grab the phone and look at him. The part of me that loves him aches inside.

"Hey Felix," Cameron says, and I can hear the smile in his voice. "I am so sorry I am not there. I guess Daddy told you we've had a row, like you and Jamie do some times."

Felix is nodding and I am mindlessly stirring the pasta sauce and trying not to let the tears well at the sound of Cameron, measured and calm and easy as he basically says exactly the same thing to Felix as I did, reassuring him, being honest but not confusing him.

We're still on the same page.

Surely that's not what I should expect from a liar like Cameron.

Camo

I finish speaking to Felix and tuck my phone away in my back pocket. I know I should have called him sooner but I wasn't sure how Ethan was going to behave. Which is stupid, because Ethan is a grown up and a decent man. No matter how he feels about me he will do exactly the right thing for Felix.

It's amazing how this whole thing seems to have derailed my view of myself and my husband, altering my perception of things I was so sure of only a few days ago.

I can't let that happen. I can't assume Ethan hates me and it is all over. I have to try and fix this. I have a chance to fix this because Ethan is good, there is mercy there to throw myself upon.

"Camo, Edwards wants to debrief," Stat calls to me from across the training room and with reluctance I drag myself through to the briefing room.

Stat takes a seat at the conference table, his fingers fly over his tablet and the wall screen activates with Janus's feed. Snipe and Blue sit side by side opposite us and Edwards enters with Berk, taking his place at the head of the table while Berk folds his frame into the seat next to me.

His scruff is already growing back but it will be a while before he has a full beard. He's going to be like a bear with a sore head while it grows back in.

"Okay," Edwards rubs a hand over his head, "Well that was a cluster fuck and a half wasn't it?"

"I take full responsibility," I speak up immediately, "I chose the wrong combination of assets for the breach, and then when things went wrong I went back myself when I should have taken back up."

Edwards waits to see if I have more to add.

Stat speaks before I can. "We underestimated the number of guards in the compound and we seriously underestimated their electronic surveillance measures. That's on me. I should have taken the time to get the equipment to check heat signatures and a scanner to monitor their comms."

"Our reconnaissance was not up to standard," Blue chimes in, "I was eager to get and get out. We did a recce but saw nothing that conflicted with the briefing document, it looked like a poorly guarded seaside home. I should have checked further."

"Anyone else want to throw themselves on their swords?" Edwards asks in a tired voice.

"I regret that I didn't get to kill anybody." Snipe says mournfully.

Edwards glares at him.

"So we have lousy teamwork, poor reconnaissance, and equipment issues."

"We do, however, have a completed role." Janus's tone over the speaker is even. "It appears that despite rumours of international involvement there is nobody for the former supporters of August Brown to rally behind. His death has, as we anticipated, thrown the opposition into disarray. Fake news on social media is already declining as there is little point in keeping it running when the beneficiary is a rapidly cooling corpse. The cult of personality is always a poor substitute for a real cause if one is trying to alter public opinion in a lasting way."

I see Stat smother a smile at Janus's phrasing.

"Well that is something I suppose," Edwards says, "Do they have anyone else they can slot into the role before the election."

"No." Janus's reply is unequivocal. "They put all their efforts towards Brown. He has been groomed for this for the last five years. He doesn't even have an appropriately compelling widow to take up the slack."

"What is international opinion regarding the death and the unfortunate footage of the team?"

"Concorde is a small Caribbean island, very few people care. The last earthquake in Haiti got knocked off the front pages in under twenty four hours and thousands died there. There were a flurry of op-ed pieces on USA black ops in the day following the role but it's hard to get enraged when there is a decent man in charge of the country and such strides have been made by him over recent years."

That's something of a relief.

"I have taken the precaution of attaching a replicating virus to every copy of the footage I can find online," Janus adds, "It degrades the video quality every time it is shared, making the footage more and more grainy. Given the sloppy way journalists get their material these days it will be a black screen within a day. I cannot do anything about the original footage though, not without expending considerable time and effort."

"I'm sure you covered our tracks as much as possible when we left the country." Stat says, and I detect the note of respect in his voice. Takes a computer expert to know a computer expert I suppose. It's all lost on me. I have to beg Ethan's help everytime I get a new phone. At the thought of him my chest aches, and I swallow against a sudden surge of loss.

"I covered you as best I could," Janus is saying, "Although the delay in sounding the compromise alert hampered me somewhat. I can't guarantee you won't be traced back to the USA."

"They can't prove anything though?" Edwards asks.

"No," Janus sounds confident, "Those high up in Concorde may suspect if they dig deep enough, but there is no proof."

"Okay." Edwards sounds like he is about to start winding up. "There are lessons to be learned here, serious ones. Whilst I'm not attaching blame to any individual this was not our finest hour and I include myself in that. I'm standing this team down while we go over resources."

Snipe growls, and Blue's face goes blank as he hides his displeasure.

Berk rolls his eyes at me, and Stat doesn't appear to care.

I feel like a failure.

"Go and relax gentlemen," Edwards says as he stands up, "And Camo, I'd like a word."

I think I am about to acquire a new asshole. Good, I deserve it.

Resolutely I follow Edwards into his small and ridiculously neat office. I stay standing as he takes a seat. Being the good military man I am, I keep my gaze two inches above his right shoulder.

"I'm prepared to offer my resignation, Sir."

"Don't fucking Sir me, this isn't the cock sucking navy."

If I had more of a death wish I'd make some crack about the marines, but I want to make it up with my husband, and I need to be alive for that.

"What I want to know, Camo, is when did you stop trusting anyone but yourself?"

I let my eyes flicker to his face. He looks pissed off as hell.

"I don't understand."

"You were support staff, you worked with Handlers and Witnesses, you were rock solid. You should be able to do this job with your hands tied behind your back and yet there you are trying to take it all on and not trusting your men's capabilities. This isn't a one man show, this is a team, with a helluva range of skills. Why aren't you letting them use them? And will you damn well sit down."

I lower myself into the chair in front of me.

Edwards looks at me, assessing me, his brow creased. "I know that there are monsters amongst our men. You know that too. But they are our monsters. And we have to trust them to stay on our side. We have trained them to be on our side. I have just shut your team down, something we both know does not sit well with the likes of Blue and Snipe, they need the roles, they need the kills."

He's right, it's the roles we take on that keep the strange psychology of our unit functioning.

"Don't think Stat and Berk are hunky dory standing down either. They need the roles too, for their own reasons. As do you. You all get something you need from this job, and you also all get to have a life outside of it."

I nod, thinking about trust. I didn't trust my team and I didn't trust my husband. I think it's time that changed.

"I suggest that you try and sort things out with Ethan," Edwards says quietly, "Secrecy is important, for sure, but trust is more important. Try and show him some, after all the secret is well and truly out of the bag now!"

Chapter Six

Ethan

It's nine a.m., Felix has just left for school and I am tidying his room. I want to get a load of washing on before I leave for my practice. I'm working eleven to seven today.

My phone starts ringing. Cameron's jaunty tune - The Beach Boys, Kokomo - sets my nerves on edge. I'm not in the mood for this. Felix was a pain in the ass last night, insisting on sleeping with me and snoring like a warthog - how a small boy can sound like that is beyond me.

I have a full roster of patients today and I have to pick up Felix from his after school club before I start dinner for us. I have a feeling it's going to be takeout again tonight.

The phone stops ringing.

I breathe a sigh of relief and walk through into our bedroom, swiping yesterday's pants and shirt off the chaise by the window.

Two seconds later the phone starts again.

"Have you any idea how fucking annoying that is." I am yelling into the speaker. "It's fucking passive aggressive stalking shit, you dickhead."

"Sorry, I thought maybe you didn't have time to get to it."

"Then I would have called you back."

"Or you're ignoring me."

"I'm ignoring you."

"Badly."

"I will improve." I lean my head back against the bedroom wall. Our big wooden bed is dressed with the dark grey sheets and covers that I know he likes. I had planned a welcome home loving that was going to blow his mind. And mine. I squeeze my eyes shut against the betrayal. I don't even know if what I thought about that was real anymore. Maybe I wasn't a man who could drive him to the heights of pleasure, maybe it was all a lie.

"I can hear you thinking."

"Yeah, I'm thinking you fucked up everything I thought I knew."

I hear him sigh. "I know, but we need to talk, we can't leave it like this."

"Can't we?" I say, "It's the old old story. Boy meets boy, boy loves boy, boy lies like a rug, boy gets told to fuck right off. End of story. What's to talk about?"

"I've never seen you angry before the other day."

"Don't change the subject."

"I'm not, I get it, but I think it's important that in all the time I have known you I never saw you mad before. That's got to count for something. I can't be that much of an asshole."

"Maybe you were really good at placating me."

"Maybe we just worked, and that's why you never needed to be mad."

"We'll never know," I say bitterly, "It wasn't the real you."

"It was."

"And now you are trying to gaslight me."

"No, I'm not trying to pretend I didn't lie, but that me, me with you, that was the most real I ever got. Please don't let it be over."

I don't want it to be over but I don't know how to move forward.

I woke up this morning hard as a rock from dreams of being fucked by my big bad secret agent husband. Two strokes of my cock and I was coming over my own hand.

The thought disgusts me now. I've never been that kind of a man. Violence is the absolute last resort and whilst I know how to hurt a human body I can't begin to think why I would want to.

Yet some horrible deep dark corner of my psyche finds the thought of Cameron being that kind of a man ridiculously sexy.

"Can I come over?"

Cameron sounds like he used to, years ago, when we were first getting together and I didn't want him to meet Felix until I was sure he would go the distance. He used to call me late at night, after Felix was in bed, his voice warm, his desire to see me in every syllable.

I check the time on the phone. Maybe a time limited meeting is a good way to start this, hash out the practicalities, see the lay of the land.

"I have to be at work by eleven."

"I can work with that, I'll see you soon."

I disconnect the call and hear the front door open, typical Cameron, he must have been outside all the time.

I steel myself for a difficult conversation and a fight with my own libido because chances are a penitent Cameron will be even hotter than Alpha Cameron.

Talking sternly to myself I gather up the laundry pile. I am not going to just roll over on this, I love him to death but this is massive, this has implications I probably haven't even thought of yet.

Carrying the pile of laundry I make my way down the stairs. "We need to get the practical issues sorted out first, Cameron..."

Two men are looking up at me, they are wearing dark tight fitting pants and long sleeve tshirts with back vests over the top, their faces are covered by balaclavas but I can see the pale skin around their eyes. It makes them look like ghouls.

Not for a second do I consider this a robbery.

Not with Cameron at the forefront of my mind.

I drop the laundry and turn to run back up the stairs, my foot slips on a tshirt, one of my knees slams into the hard wood of the stairs as a hand grabs my ankle. I twist onto my back, kicking out. I feel my heel connect with flesh and there is a grunt.

I grab for the banister, trying to pull myself upright but they are both on me. All I can see is black cloth and their combined weight holds me against the stairs, the treads cutting into my back. I don't even get a chance to yell. There is a sting at my neck and everything starts to go fuzzy, the edges of my vision flaring white.

Then nothing.

Camo

Ethan's car is in the driveway, I wonder what the protocol is now, do I knock on the front door or can I let myself in?

I'm still thinking about it when I get to the door.

It's ajar.

He wouldn't have left it open for me, that's stupid.

Felix wouldn't have left it open, he goes out the kitchen door at the side.

The hairs on the back of my neck rise.

Keeping to one side I push the door open, peering around. Clothing is scattered down the stairs in front of me. I recognise Ethan's favourite heather grey t-shirt, the one he refuses to throw out. His comfort t-shirt he calls it. He wears it when he's feeling down. I've been trying to find a replacement for it, it's more holes than shirt now.

I step into the house.

There is that sense of emptiness, that sense of violence done and gone. It's not something you can point a finger at but in my job you get to know it when you feel it.

"Ethan!" I call out.

Never assume though, I've been wrong before, I got sucker punched as a tadpole because I didn't properly check if a room was clear. That stung.

I move through the house, checking out the windows every chance I get, he might be outside, he might be in the greenhouse.

I know he isn't.

"Ethan, it's me," I shout again.

It's not good, it's definitely not good.

I start up the stairs. Something gold glitters against the wood halfway up. Keeping a wary eye open I bend and pick up Ethan's starfish necklace. The chain has snapped. I slip it into my pocket and reach for my phone as I continue to move upstairs.

Everything is silent. I feel a trickle of sweat run down my back under my shirt.

I glance down at the phone and open my short list of contacts.

Felix's room is empty, his bed neatly made.

Our room is the same. I notice the dark grey linen on the bed, Ethan always puts that on when he wants to play. He thinks with his colouring he look good against the grey. He's right.

Nothing. Nobody.

I don't hesitate in calling the compromised code this time. I hit the name Applejack on my contact list.

Edwards answers on the first ring. "What is it?"

"Ethan has been taken."

"Where is Felix?"

"Fuck, school, he should be in school, it was his day to ride the bus."

"Check, I'll get Janus on this now."

My hands are shaking as I scroll to the number of Felix's school. It rings for an interminable time. I try to take slow deep breaths, shut down the unwelcome images in my brain, focus on the facts.

Between the time I got off the phone to Ethan and arrived at the house was under 15 minutes, I'd been loitering in a coffee shop nearby working up the balls to call him.

"Hello, how can I help?" Finally someone answers the phone.

"Hi," I'm amazed my voice comes out so normal. "This is Cameron Green, Felix's Dad, I was wondering if he made it to school today. He was feeling a bit under the weather yesterday and my husband wasn't sure he was going to make it. It's my turn to pick him up and I can't get hold of Ethan."

The lies trip off my tongue, my voice light, just the faintest touch of an exasperated and busy professional father.

"I'll just check for you now, Mr Green."

"Thanks so much."

There is a pause and I roll on the balls of my feet. The adrenaline is spiking in me, I feel it in the prickle of the skin on the back of my hands. I hold my nose and blow, alleviating the effects on my system.

"No, Felix didn't make it in today."

"Okay, thanks for checking, I'd better get my butt home, I imagine my husband is up to his neck in what usually comes out of sick little boys."

She laughs, "Amazing where it all comes from isn't it!" Clearly a mom herself.

"Thanks again," I say and cut the call. I'm hitting Applejack again before I know what my fingers are doing. "Felix too."

"On it," Edwards snaps, "Get back here, I'm calling everyone in."

I walk out to my truck, carefully pulling the door shut behind me. I climb into the cab and clutch the steering wheel with all my strength, my knuckles white, the latte I gulped in town churning in my guts.

I wish I was like my team, too damaged to care, then I could maybe deal with this better, because with this level of terror inside me I'm no use to anyone. I didn't know it was possible to feel this scared.

Ethan

I wake with a strange sense of pressure in my ears and the sound of a low thrumming. Everything is hot and black and for a moment I panic, every muscle tensing.

My breathing goes haywire and I gasp for breath. I feel fabric against my lips, my face, my fluttering eyelashes. There is a hood over my head.

My hands are restrained in front of me.

Where the fuck am I?

There is pressure again and my ears pop.

I'm on a plane.

Memory comes back online.

I was walking downstairs, there were strangers in the house. I remember falling, kicking out, I remember a stinging prick at my neck.

My mouth is dry, my head aches. I've been drugged and now I am in a plane and we're coming into land somewhere.

The plane rocks.

Small plane, buffeted by turbulence, not as well pressurised as a commercial liner. It must have been the changing pressure that woke me up.

The soft dark fabric of the hood against my face keeps threatening to tip me over into panic. I hate my face being covered.

I take shallow breaths.

The plane wallows again and then there is a bump and the noise gets louder as the engines roar. The plane vibrates and I am pushed against the seatbelt straps as it slows.

The plane slows further and then stops. There are muffled sounds as someone stands and then I hear the heavy thunk as the door is opened. Even though the cloth hood I can feel the damp heat of the tropics.

It fills my senses. Screaming cicadas, the smell of rotting vegetation, wet clay and recent rain.

I was knocked out in a civilised suburb of Washington DC and I wake up in the tropics. My sense of place feels disjointed. I am adrift, confused.

Where the hell am I?

What the hell is going on?

A hard grasp on my forearm pulls me to my feet. "I know you are awake, you can walk, I'm not carrying you."

I stumble, unsure where to place my feet.

I hear someone else say "We're going to have to carry the kid, he won't move."

My heart stutters in my chest. I try to pull away from whoever has a grasp on me. Felix is here, they have Felix too.

I might want to fall apart, but now I won't.

Camo

"How the fuck did they find me? How the fuck did they find my husband?" That's the only thing I seem capable of saying.

Stat is at his computer console, he hasn't moved in the hours since I got back to the farm. Janus's live connection is a straight violet line across the black screen, he's there but he's not talking, he's elsewhere in the webs between worlds, bringing his resources to bear to track down Ethan.

"We'll find him, Camo." Edwards tries to reassure me but his energy is dark and grim as he stands in the middle of the room, his feet planted wide as if preparing to withstand a flood.

Blue is pacing back and forth, a thin sheen of sweat across his forehead. It looks like he has been dragging his hands through his normally neat hair.

I want to hit something, I want to break something. In my head a clock is ticking. It started the moment I walked into our house. This waiting is going to break me.

This has never happened before. Not in the Handler system, not here. Nobody has ever found those we care about.

It was always a possibility though.

Berk is sitting at one of the desks, his head in his hands. Snipe is hovering beside him and I can see the twitching nerves in him too, his hands making fists and then releasing as if he needs something in them.

All these men are showing how much this matters, none of them have left the room, and yet most of them have never even met Ethan.

Ethan is the dream, Ethan is normal, Ethan is what they protect although they will never have it.

Stat turns away from the computer. "It seems most likely it was the last role," he says. "We've never been so close to being caught before, it has to be that."

"I have a trace," Janus's voice comes over the speaker.

The muscles in my shoulders flex. Here we go. Give me something to do.

"I have a lead, but there is something else."

"What is it?" Edwards takes point.

Janus' voice changes, less imperious, more formal. "I regret to inform you that I have picked up a live feed online. Someone clearly wanted us to find it. It was darkweb but keyed with DEA and NSA code words. My searches picked it up before they did but..."

"What is it," Stat's tone is surprisingly gentle, as if he feels he needs to coax this information from Janus.

"It's the abductee, they have him on a live feed."

"Show me." I can feel a tightness in my chest, like my heart is being squeezed. I know what is coming.

"I'm sorry..."

"Put it on the fucking screen."

The main screen above Stat flickers to life.

Ethan hangs by his wrists which are tied to a pole above his head. He is naked, his body streaked with sweat and dirt. His bare feet barely touch the cement floor beneath him.

Two men are beating him.

There is no sound but I can imagine the meaty impact of their fists on his pale body. He takes a blow to the solar plexus. I see him clutch the ropes around his wrists and draw his knees up, swinging as more blows land.

The room is well lit and Ethan's body in all it's vulnerability is all too easy to see. The floor beneath his feet is uneven concrete, the walls behind him just bare blockwork. The beam he is tied to looks to be an old scaffolding pole.

The men back off and Ethan hangs in the ropes, his head down, his hair drenched with sweat, his rib cage rising and falling rapidly. Blood mixed with saliva from a split lip drips down onto his chest.

One man steps forward and grabs Ethan's hair, twisting his head up so we can see his face. He grimaces in pain. He bares his teeth and they are red with blood.

"More." There is a terrible eagerness in the voice that comes out of camera shot.

A fist impacts Ethan's face and I watch the bloody saliva spray from his lips.

Something inside me tries to explode. I cry out my rage and despair and turn towards the wall, my arm pulling back. I need to hit something, hurt something, preferably myself.

Berk moves before I can smash my hand to pieces on the wall. My punch hits Berk's open palm and his huge hand closes around my fist, wrapping it, smothering it. I look up into his black eyes. Eyes that have seen so much pain and given it too. I feel his empathy, his understanding.

"We got you." He enfolds me in his massive arms, holding me against his chest, and I want to cry. "You are not alone. We will bring him home."

Chapter Seven

Ethan

Physical pain I can live with, it gives me something to focus on. See the blow coming, anticipate it. Feel it, breathe into it, let the pain it spawns run its course. Keep breathing as it ebbs.

Fear is what will take me down.

I can't let fear in because somewhere there is Felix and he is going to need me.

A blow to my solar plexus has me drawing my knees up as a reflex and I gasp. My body goes haywire for a second, pain and no air and the fear starts to sink into my mind.

No!

I force myself to inhale. I hang in the ropes, panting, sweaty and filthy, aching all over. Blood from my mouth drips onto my chest.

They haven't asked me a thing and that's not right, surely.

You don't beat the living shit out of someone just for funsies, or maybe you do.

This is about Cameron, it has to be. And yet they haven't asked me a thing about him. Which means information isn't the purpose of this.

This is theatre.

I'm naked. They stripped my clothes off me and strung me up before they ever took the bag off my head. They don't care if I see them. They don't care if I see where I am.

This is a message to my husband.

Thank god Felix isn't seeing this.

I try not to think about what he is seeing, what is happening to him.

There is no point in wasting a motivating factor a logical part of my mind insists. They will save him for something else. Your job is to endure. To be ready when the time comes to act.

A hand is twisted in my hair and my face lifted.

"More," says the praying mantis figure that calls the shots from the edge of the room. His voice is high and reedy, horribly eager.

The men who beat me are professionals, their eyes dead, their punches measured, causing pain but designed to be sustained. They treat my body like a workout.

Their faces swim before me, one is tall with a twisted nose broken more than once. His stance is solid, weight on his toes. He wears a shoulder holster over his long sleeved tee. The other is shorter, stockier, breathing more heavily and he grunts as he puts his weight behind his punches.

I tell people every day how to deal with pain, severe pain, lost limbs, old injuries, twisted scars and shattered joints.

I wrap my hands around the ropes that my wrists, protecting the joints.

In my head is a deep blue pool, the surface reflects a night sky. I slip into the pool and tell every muscle to relax. Roll with the punches sings the mantra in my head.

Light explodes but it seems far away as I look up at it through the dark surface of the pool in my mind I shelter in.

The pain is distant and manageable.

I will endure.

It is not a choice, it is a fact.

Camo

"The trail is a mile wide, it's clearly a trap." Janus's voice is his usual mix of haughty and impatient. "There was a private plane on diplomatic clearance booked out of DCA with a flight plan logged for Concorde less than half an hour after Camo called in the alert."

"Does that mean their president is involved?" Blue asks, "Normally only heads of state get diplomatic clearance."

"Not necessarily," Stat says, "Although he could be placating the opposition to show he wasn't involved, and if there is a USA link to the assassination it wasn't at his request. My guess is he's going for transparency."

"So who was on board?" Edwards prowls back and forth behind Stat at his console.

"No APIS is required for diplomatic clearance into the USA." Janus replies. "And I doubt Concorde has a manifest logged either. It would take me too long to hack the security cameras at the airport, do we have any other clues?"

"Pull up the footage of the feed," Snipe says, "Maybe we can pick something up from that."

I turn my back to the screens where my husband suffers because I'm fucking spineless.

The room goes silent as they watch longer than I could bear to.

"Tall guy that walked into camera there on the side, the one in the suit, blow him up, let's see if we can get more detail." Blue snaps out.

"Your wish is my command, Indigo!" Janus's voice drips sarcasm.

Stat hums out a conciliatory sound.

"Sorry, Blue."

I risk a glance over my shoulder at the screens.

On the far right of the screen a tall angular shape makes little effort to hide.

Blue looks back at me, "Recognise him?"

It's the guy who was out on the balcony the day Blue and I recce'd the beachside house. I recognise the elongated angles of his body.

"Yes," I say. "He was at the villa, could he be the brother?"

"Checking," Janus says. There is a pause. "Yes, that is Damas Brown, also known as Damas Cristoph, illegitimate brother of August Brown."

"Find him." I want his head on a plate, I want to feed him to lions, I want my husband out of his hands.

"On it." Stat's voice has new energy.

"What do you see as the purpose of this, Janus?" Edwards asks.

"In my opinion the intention is to get Camo to the island. The live feed is the first salvo in a war of psychological pressure. They want Camo and I don't think it is about revenge. I believe they want a confession, freely given."

"The President will likely resign if he is implicated strongly enough in the killing of his opponent," Blue says, "Hell, he's decent enough that he may resign anyway if they can prove it was done for him if not by him! He's that kind of guy."

"That will likely postpone the election, give the opposition time to regroup, and if they have a confession and an American national as the guilty party they could get a sea slug elected."

"Additionally, a freely given confession from Camo will bloody the nose of the US administration, and that will please the Chinese no end."

Janus is right.

"What about Felix?" I ask.

"I imagine that Felix will be the next tool to be used."

The tension in the room rises at Janus's words.

"I have a private jet standing by at Ronald Regan," Stat says, "We can be at Guadeloupe in just over four hours. And a private helicopter can be waiting there for us, we can fast rope into wherever they are."

Snipe just gets up and leaves the room, Berk follows him.

"Can you get us a location in that time, Janus?" Blue asks.

"Naturally, I am already 80% sure where they have Camo's husband and son. I will have schematics and a ground plan by the time you board."

"Make it so, I will run point," Edwards turns and walks towards his office, "I have to update some contacts."

Stat is opening drawers and gathering equipment, earpieces and scanners, wrist computers and night vision scopes. Blue joins him, and they start to argue about the best jammer for what they expect to face.

The thing that amazes me is that there are no questions, no vacillating. The team just swings into action, assuming that we will all act together to bring Ethan home.

I want to say something. To thank them. I am so humbled that despite all my shortcomings as a leader they are with me on this.

I clear my throat.

Blue looks up at me. "Don't say it," he advises, "It's not even worth saying. We don't even think about it, only you alpha leader types think about it. We're used to assholes, and you're our asshole. What you fight we fight."

I manage a crumpled smile.

He smiles back at me, surprisingly sweet. "And of course we never turn down the opportunity to kill people," he adds.

The day I met Ethan my shoulder was aching like a bitch. The wound was healed but the tissue and nerve damage under the skin was making sleeping hard and working out impossible. I was antsy with inactivity, moody with pain, and feeling sorry for myself. No stranger to the evils of physio I was not looking forward to starting therapy but knew it would pay off in the end.

Slouched in a chair in the waiting room of an upmarket private clinic I was at least glad our insurance got us the best when we needed it. I'd filled in the questionnaire putting a shoulder impalement during diving as the cause of the injury - it had been similar, the bullet had entered the fleshy part of my shoulder from above. If I hadn't been wearing the vest it would have been a through and through. As it was, the kevlar stopped the exit and the bullet got stuck causing damage to the nerves.

"Dr Ethan will see you now." I was shown into a sunlit room with an examination couch, a plethora of plants and a slim, red headed man in yoga pants, wearing a wide smile.

I wasn't fooled. I've had physio from elf like girls who could double as sadistic mistresses and had hands with the kind of grip you found on a drill sergeant. Dr Ethan looked gentle enough but I had poor hopes of getting out of here without calling on my reserves of manliness.

Turned out I was wrong. Dr Ethan was the exception that proves the rule. He was thorough but gentle, his hands were firm but his voice and his eyes kept me distracted from any pain. I melted under them, and as everyone knows a relaxed patient is a good patient.

By the end of the session I would have laid down my life for him.

As I put my shirt back on my shoulder already felt better and I was looking forward to a decent night's sleep.

"Are you some sort of miracle worker?" I asked as I tested the more mobile joint.

"Not at all," he said, "You are just a really good patient, most big guys like you tend to tense when a man touches them but you didn't, it helped with the process."

I smirked and puffed my chest out, he saw I was a big guy.

"I'm really not averse to being touched by another man," I said.

He actually blushed, his creamy skin turning a glowing red across his cheeks, and his dark eyelashes fluttered. "That's useful to know," he said quietly.

Physio was looking a lot more enticing than it had before, I was starting to hope this would be a lengthy process.

Fortunately it wasn't lengthy because Dr Ethan refused to date me until my treatment was finished. He would flirt and chat and the eye fucks were a big part of our sessions but he wouldn't let me take him to dinner until we were done.

When he finally signed me off as fit I had him up against the wall of his office before the ink was dry on his signature and was kissing the breath out of him.

From then on our relationship progressed in leaps and bounds.

The first night he let me take him to bed I knew I'd never want another man.

I'd had fucks that were like warfare, kisses that were battles to the end, all clashing teeth and dueling tongues. I'd had guys that fumbled in the dark and guys that knew every trick in the book and sucked my brains out through my dick. And then I laid a hand on Ethan and he trembled and the world changed.

His skin overlaying long lean muscles fascinated me. It had a lustre to it, almost a plasticity. The feel of it drove me wild. The freckles scattered across it entranced me. But more than anything was the way he responded to me, like no one had ever made him feel like that before, and maybe they hadn't.

He was nerve ends all over and I could take him apart with a kiss.

There was a truth in Ethan. Every response was heartfelt and real.

By the morning of the first night we spent together I wanted to ask him to marry me and I dared to dream I could have it all with him.

I am beginning to realise that I made a colossal mistake in not trusting Ethan from the word go.

He might never have married me if I had but he sure as hell wouldn't be hanging from a beam being beaten senseless if I had told him everything.

He might even have loved me enough to marry me anyway and he would definitely have been better prepared for the fallout I never realised my work would bring to his door.

I let my head fall back against the heavily padded seat of the private jet as it barrels south through the thin air high above commercial routes. I am an idiot. I never saw any of this coming and I should have.

In my head the same picture circulates endlessly, my husband, beaten and bloodied. I would sell my soul to swap places with him, take the pain he is being given.

Please, don't let him be dead. I pray to a god I never had to believe in before. *Please let him be alive so our contract isn't done.*

I'm sure I would feel it if our contract was done, dissolving in death, and I can still feel him there, inside my heart.

I hang onto that thought.

Chapter Eight

Ethan

The door of the small concrete room they have locked me in opens. I press my back against the wall and push myself upright. Being kicked when I am down sounds unappealing.

At least they have given me a ragged shirt and shorts to wear. It makes me feel more human, and confirms that the naked beating was very much staged. Not that is didn't hurt, it really fucking did, but the extra touches were designed to incite, to enrage passions, to get people to make mistakes in anger.

"How are you Mr Green?" The tall thin figure that orchestrated the beating steps into the room. He's followed by a slight young man with an asian look about him, carrying an open laptop. By the expression on his face he is no more happy to be here than I am. "Are you ready for your next scene in front of the camera?"

"Who are you?" I don't know if it is necessary to know but I'd like to, for when we get out of this.

"I'm Mr Brown," he says, smiling like a skull, his skin stretched tight over the bones of his face. "That's funny isn't it, you're Mr Green and I'm Mr Brown, we could be starring in a Tarantino movie."

"Some of us are, and you got the Director's role"

"Oh, that's funny, you're very sharp aren't you."

"I'd like to see my son," I say pleasantly.

"All in good time, all in good time."

I wonder what they have planned for me next.

"I'll tell you a secret," Mr Brown says, moving further into the room, "It's a very good job that husband of yours killed my brother because I doubt even I could keep him from that boy of yours. So pretty, so delicate. Just how he used to like them, may he rest in peace."

Over his shoulder I see his companion swallow convulsively. No, he really isn't happy to be here.

"Don't worry, Mr Green, nothing awful is going to happen to you or your boy now, we're saving that for the last act." He motions his companion forward. "My associate here is just going to film you reading a message to your husband and then he is going to post it where we are sure he will see it. I am sure he will see sense in the matter, he's the hero type after all isn't he."

"Uh, I need you to read what is on the screen." There is a sheen of sweat over the Asian guy's face, and his hands as he turns the laptop to face me are trembling. I can see the tension in the tendons of his narrow wrists where they protrude from the sleeves of his white shirt.

I could break those wrists, I know how.

"Why are you doing this?" I ask him.

Brown assumes I am speaking to him. "Because we need to win an election, and we need your husband to admit his guilt for that. Then I can step into my dear late brother's place and despite my less than stellar birth I will be elected."

"Not you," I snap, "You." I look the young guy in the eyes. "He's taken my son, a little boy, he's threatening us. What are you doing here? You don't look like you are part of this."

"Not, I'm not." He takes a step back, shaking his head. "I'm just the computer guy, I didn't know."

Brown's skeletal hand comes down on the young man's shoulder. "You are part of this now, I suggest you do your part."

The young man swallows, his eyes darting to mine. He lifts the laptop again.

"Online activities have real world consequences," I say to him, "Remember that."

I scan the words on the screen. It's a message direct to Cameron, begging him to hand himself in or Felix and I will suffer horribly. It's sickening rather than emotional. If I have to read how he intends to do to Felix and I there is a chance I will throw up.

"Bring me to my son and I'll read it, but not these words. I can't say this in front of a child."

"You are not in a position to bargain."

"Maybe not, but I can sell this message if I do it voluntarily and I'm not doing that without seeing Felix. I know my husband, I know what will make him act."

"Really?"

"Yes, really. It's thanks to my lying prick of a husband that my son and I are here. I don't give a flying fuck what happens to him now but I've been married to him long enough to know how to manipulate him. Bring me to my son and I'll sell this story for you, and then you let us go."

He pretends to consider it. I pretend to believe him.

"Maybe it would look better if the two of you were together. Maybe we need more emotional triggers. You with your boy, you begging into the camera while your child trembles with fear in his piss stained pants. I could see that working."

He's getting carried away with his own twisted vision, he's been inciting people online too long or maybe he's taking the Tarantino analogy too far. But if it buys me time.

"I like the way you think, Mr Green, you have a sadistic streak all your own." he turns to the Asian guy. "Go set up a better camera in the villa, get some lights on it. Let's make a movie." He laughs at his own joke, turning his back on me and moving towards the door.

I know the vital places where his vertebrae meet his skull. I know where the nerves in his neck cross and are sensitive to pressure.

I could do it now, but I have patience, I need Felix first.

Camo

"Damas Brown has been building a house for himself in the interior, in virgin jungle. It does not appear totally finished but there are other buildings on site and it is very out of the way. I believe he has Ethan and Felix there." Janus's voice over the connection to the plane is clear as a bell.

The image of a building flickers onto the screen on the bulkhead. It's brutal in its modernism. Three stories of dark grey featureless concrete with slab like balconies and a rectangular swimming pool in front. The roof is covered with solar panels and a satellite array.

It looks unwelcoming and totally at odds with the dense jungle around it.

The red earth around it is scared and rutted from machinery, the tracks filled with soupy puddles from recent rain.

"Not my idea of paradise," Stat says.

"Money doesn't get you taste," says Snipe wisely.

"How close can a helicopter get us without alerting them?"

"There's a fair bit of helicopter activity in the area, the regatta has resumed and they have eye in the sky reporting." Stat says, "I reckon we can get within five hundred metres if we go in low to the ridge behind the house."

"Exit plans?"

"Working on it." Blue unstraps from his seat and huddles next to Stat, the two of them pouring over satellite photos.

"The copter pilot in Guadeloupe is a friend of a friend," Edwards voice comes over the comms. "He knows this is an operation and he's up for it."

"Any experience?"

"Flew in Afghanistan then moved to drones, didn't like it and retired, doesn't like ferrying tourists around any better."

"Are we recruiting?" Snipe asks.

"Fuck no, I've got enough ex military on my hands."

"Landing in twenty minutes, gentleman." The pilot informs us. "We're being directed to a hangar on the far edge of the airfield."

"Roger that."

There is no point in flying a flag about this, we need to try and be low key for all Edwards and his contacts are calling in favours across the Caribbean, getting us airspace clearance and schmoozing officials to look the other way.

I feel calmer now. I'm doing something. I'm going to get Ethan and Felix out and my team is with me, all the way.

"*Call me Ralph, just Ralph,*" is our helicopter pilot, he's a rangy man with a porn star moustache and a tropical tan.

He clearly misses the old days as he swoops low across the channel from Guadeloupe and towards the north end of Concorde.

"Anything I should know?" he asks, "Will I have to start throwing this around the sky?"

"Maybe ground to air but we're aiming to neutralise everything," Stat tells him, "I'll link you in on comms."

"It's good to be back," he settles his ass into his seat and he has a steely look in his eye as we circle the tip of Concorde and go in over the east coast which has higher cliffs and dense jungle.

Ralph holds the bird steady above a clearing in the jungle as Blue, Stat, Berk and I fast rope down. Snipe stays in the copter, his TAC-50 set up on the floor of the surprisingly roomy cabin of Eurocopter AS350.

The sun is up, the light is good, it's a blue sky day in the Caribbean and I'm going to kill the man who hurt my Ethan.

Stat leads the way, his wrist computer guiding him with GPS to bring us over the ridge behind the concrete monstrosity of Green's villa.

Satellite coverage has a worker's shack to the east of the main house, Janus is confident that Ethan's beating was filmed there, but whether he is still there is unknown.

First place we try though.

Despite the jammers Stat has at his disposal we're not going to be blocking comms, we need anyone in the house to be unaware until the last minute, and given their tech capabilities so far they are likely used frequently, a drop out would be noticed.

We break the head of the ridge and in the distance I can see the dots of the regatta boats out on the white capped sea. The roof of the house is below us, it's array of solar panels sparkling in the sunlight, sucking up the energy.

The house is off grid and the only land entry is over a dirt track over two miles long. We're well inside their perimeter from the word go.

It's heavy going down towards the house. The ground under our boots is slick wet red earth that clings and clumps. We're tramping through pretty much virgin jungle, clearly gardens aren't a big thing in the guy who designed this place.

The ground levels out and Blue holds up a hand. We press ourselves into the sharp shadows, thinking like trees, being part of the wall of vegetation as two men in fatigues patrol the edge of the cleared land around the house. They pass a cigarette between them. They don't even glance towards the jungle.

I look at Blue, a question in my expression. He reads it, and shakes his head. He could take them out but it's not necessary just yet. Ethan and Felix first, then playtime.

Stat indicates to the left and we move quietly along the edges of the jungle. I see a small block built shack tucked at the far end of the cleared land. It has a tin roof and a single window cover with plywood. The sun is full on it. It must be like a fucking sauna in there.

The rear of the shack has another window, again covered with plywood, nailed in place.

Berk steps forward, his massive hands going to the edges of the wood. The muscles in his arms bulge, there is a crack as the wood comes away from the wall.

I peer inside.

Ethan has his hand thrown up to shade his eyes from the sudden sunlight. He's sitting on the cement floor and he is squinting, trying to make out what is happening.

"Ethan, it's me." It's not the most polished rescue phrase but the smile that breaks over his face is like the sun coming up again. He scrambles to his feet.

There is a second more muted crack as Berk twists the plywood away from the window, giving me room to reach in for Ethan. He raises his arms and I grasp him firmly around the forearms, dragging him up and through the open window. His bare knees catch the rough block and he grimaces but makes no noise.

I haul him into the open air. He looks up at me, the full light of the sun on his face. Bruises mar his creamy skin, his lips are puffy and split, he has a nasty looking cut over one eye.

He's alive.

He stinks.

He's gorgeous. My heart beats a frenzied tattoo of recognition and joy.

"Felix?" he asks.

"We think he's in the main house."

"Let's go."

"No, Berk will guide you back to the copter, we'll go after Felix."

His expression morphs into deep disgust. "Don't be fucking stupid," he says and moves to the edge of the shack where Stat glances back at him and flashes him a smile.

Ethan

I know the names they go by, of course I do. I have seen glimpses of their faces, blurry in the background, in the innocuous shots Cameron has sent me over the years, when he was pretending to be beneath the sea.

Now I see their personalities in their movements and I know that if I had met them before this I would have known. These men are not normal.

Blue moves like a true predator, light on his feet, a knife at his side. Berk is massive, all bulging muscles and tattoos, his black eyes swivelling as we move along the edges of the jungle towards the concrete building that rises out of the blood red mud. He feels like a bull, forceful and barely in control, violence beats from him in waves.

Stat is familiar, silent but familiar. I know the way he walks, the angle of his head as he checks his wrist computer. He puts a hand on Berks shoulder, slowing him and guides us deeper into the jungle.

"Janus just managed to hack the system of the guy who designed the house," Stat's voice is quiet, "The basement level is all utilities, ground source heat pump, battery arrays, water purification and a serious data room with built in cooling.

"We have a main entrance on the other side of the building, that comes in at level two, big entrance hall and the whole front of the building is glass, big show off space. Kitchen is at the rear, along with stairs to the third level where the guest suites are." He looks concerned. "I have no idea where they could be holding Felix. I would assume the third floor, in a suite somewhere, but it's a big open space in there and we're going to be sitting ducks if we don't know where we are going."

"Is there entry to the basement level?" Blue asks.

"There is a maintenance entrance but the stairs up from the basement are narrow, if we meet anyone on those we'll be in a bottleneck."

"The data room is in the basement you said?" I speak up.

Stat nods.

"They have a computer guy on staff, nervous, clearly doesn't want to be here. If he's there he can tell us where Felix is being held. They were in the process of setting up another movie shoot, this time with Felix and I. That was hours ago, I think he's dragging his feet because he's reluctant."

I haven't looked at Cameron since he pulled me out of the shack and tried to send me away. I don't know if I can. I don't know how to speak to him, how to think about him like this, in this situation. I focus instead on Stat.

Stat glances at the others.

Out of the corner of my eye I see Cameron nod.

With no discussion Blue moves to the front.

There is thirty yards between the edge of the jungle and the concrete wall of the house. Blue hesitates, listening, watching, and then motions us forward.

We cross the red mud and I feel more exposed than I ever have in my life.

There is a blank, anonymous door set into the concrete. Stat makes short work of its electronic lock and we slip inside.

Inside it is cool, all humming machinery and bright white floors. It smells like chemicals and bleach, spotlessly clean. My bare feet track what looks like bloody footprints on the pure white tiles.

Stat indicates a door at the far back of the space.

Cameron moves past me. I can see impatience in his step, there is an angry push to his strides now, and as he closes on the door he raises his assault rifle to his shoulder. It's so casual, so obviously practised a movement for him.

He doesn't pause at the door, he just kicks it open.

There is a brief shout of fear and I hurry forward with the others.

Pushing into the room I see the young computer guy on the floor, his suit jacket is off and his sleeves are rolled up on his pale forearms. He is face down and Cameron has a knee in his back and a hand in his hair.

"Where the hell is my son?" Cameron barks.

"I don't know, I don't know anything, I just run the tech." He grimaces with fear and pain.

Cameron turns to Blue who has an awful eager look on his face. "Make him talk."

"Please, no, I don't know anything."

"Don't hurt him." My voice comes out weak, my throat dry and burning.

"Kill him if you have to." Cameron's voice is pure steel.

Blue sways forward, moving like a cobra, his blade in his hand.

I don't know this man who I am married to, he decides on the end of someone's life without considering it for a second. He gives an order and someone moves to obey.

"No!" The young guy and I speak at the same time.

"Let him go, Cameron." I add.

A pained expression crosses my husband's face at the use of his name.

"Let him go and find our son."

Cameron jerks his head and Blue steps back, "Your lucky day, Geek," he says, "Now run. And don't scream until you are far away."

The guy scrambles to his feet, he looks at me, his eyes damp, his face white. "I delayed as long as I could," he whispers, "I said I couldn't get a good connection. I don't want this, I never signed up for this."

"I know."

"Your son, I think he's on the top level. I heard them complaining, they can't do anything with him, he just sits there."

"Go," I tell him, "Go far away, get out of this."

He scuttles for the door.

"Before you go," Stat speaks up, "How many guards in the house?"

"Two with the boy all the time. They are professionals. Another six patrol the main levels, at least ten outside but they are normal army, young, conscripts. Other than that there is just the cook and Mr Brown."

It seems being allowed to live makes people more likely to cooperate.

"Thank you." I say.

He nods, "Henry," he says, "I'm Henry Park, please remember that, in case I suffer real world consequences."

He's gone.

I turn to Cameron, "Would you have killed him?"

"It's what we do," he says with finality.

Camo

The stairs to the main level are metal and we climb them carefully, guns at the ready.

I'm in front this time.

I ease open the door at the top a fraction and listen.

I can hear two men talking to my right, their voices clearly funneling into the stairwell.

"Boss gone for his morning swim?"

"Yes, wants to get his constitutional in before showtime with the gay and the kid."

"How the hell does that work? He's gay and he's got a husband and a kid?"

"Maybe he's secretly a girl."

They laugh.

"Didn't look like a girl when you were whaling on him the other day."

"No, fair play to the little poof, he took it like a man."

I let the words settle inside me, tinder to a flame ready to burn.

These guys are not local, easy banter, no problem with dirty work, these are true mercenaries, following the money.

"Any idea what the plan is after showtime, I'm sick of staying in this concrete fortress?"

"Shoot the kid and the dad, dump them, back to town and wait for hubbie to turn up. No way will he let his loved ones go through what the boss says he is going to do."

"Thank god, I was dreading the thought of killing the kid like that. I can live with a clean shot to the head but what he said he was going to do, damn, messy."

"You know these weird voodoo types, they like a complicated death."

I can hear Ethan breathing behind me, I know it's him because he is practically panting and his hot breath is on my neck.

He's never experienced anything like this before, he's never seen me like this. I know it will change his view of me, more than my lies already have.

It's all very well knowing in the abstract that you have been lied to but when you see the reality of the other person, without their camouflage, hell he must be terrified.

I turn, expecting him to see fear in his eyes, expecting to see terror on his face, instead there is something new, something I never saw before, a grim resolve.

"Get them," he says, "We need to find our son."

I'm moving before the words have left his mouth. I shoulder the door open and I'm firing before the two men have a chance to turn. Head shots take them both down with blood spraying up the white walls.

The suppressed assault rifle produces a sound of 136Db, significantly lower than unsuppressed, but certainly not silent. Now the concrete works in our favour though, keeping the noise inside.

"Fan out," I tell the boys, "Go through this place like dysentery."

I don't care if Ethan sees me as a killer for the rest of our lives, if I can do this for him, for us, for the family we were then that's good enough for me.

I grab Ethan's hand, it feels small and hot in mine but he grips back, his fingers around mine, one firm clasp. We're on the same page again for the moment.

It's a weird feeling, him at my shoulder as we move forward. I notice his grace all over again, his strength, and every time I glance over at him I see his character clearer than I ever saw it before. He is a man, willing to fight for what he loves. It sends the adrenaline coursing through me.

Everything comes together, it's a fight the likes of which you only get in the last days of training, when you are nothing but a killing machine, honed and primed, muscle and mind and intent all welding into perfect soldiers.

The comms are clear, Stat's voice in my ear is like another brain, feeding me information.

Berk is at rear, covering our backs, when I glance back he has a rifle to his shoulder, his steps measured, his baseball cap on back to front, his eye to his sights. He spots something, the steel barrel swings, the report echoes, the fibreglass stock kicking back doesn't even move his shoulder.

Blue in front of us moves like the nightmare he is. He is armed with his usual knife, he doesn't need a gun, he doesn't like them, he never did. He likes his kills up close and personal and when he fights it is like ballet.

His hand movement stills us. We pause. I can feel Ethan beside me, quivering with eagerness.

Blue steps into an open corridor and throws his knife. I don't see the target but I hear it hit, that particular dull thud followed by a gurgle. By the time we reach the corner Blue is wiping the knife off on his combats. A man lies in a slowly spreading pool of blood. It looks black against the polished concrete floor.

A faint smile graces Blue's classically handsome face, he looks back at Berk, "Why don't you go hold the door, we'll mop up here."

Berk huffs a laugh, turning away.

Ethan steps over the corpse, moving lightly.

"Main suite straight ahead," says Stat in my ear.

Blue nods at me.

I raise my gun and glance back at Berk's retreating back, I know why Blue sent him away. One more dead kid and Berk would never come back to us.

I wouldn't make it past one.

Chapter Nine

Ethan

I have never felt like this before. Like my blood is on fire.

All I want to do is tear apart those between me and my son.

I can feel Felix in my head, a frightened little boy once more, seeing too much of the wrong thing, facing dreadful things all alone.

I will kill whoever did this.

I don't think I even notice the men falling around us. All I know is I am within the arrow head that is Cameron and his team.

We make it up the stairs to the top level and in front of us is a heavy walnut door, the wood nearly black with stain.

Cameron raises his foot and kicks in the door.

Over his shoulder I see a man struggling out of a huge sofa, trying to get to his feet. Cameron's shot sends his head back on his shoulders, blood spraying like crimson blossom.

I race into the room. The tall man with the broken nose has his arm around Felix's throat and a gun at his head. He is backing towards the floor to ceiling glass that fronts the suite. Outside I can see brilliant sunlight and the far distant sea.

"Nobody move," he says, "Or you know what happens."

Felix looks at me, his eyes are distant, far away, dreaming of some other place.

I move forward, unarmed, my hands up.

"Please," I say, my voice quavering, "Give me my son, you don't want to do this."

"I don't, but I will." His tone is adamant.

"Please," I say, "They'll lay down their weapons, just let me have my son."

The man is wearing an open neck Henley, I can see the pulse beating strongly in his neck. His arm across Felix's throat is steady as a rock. If he makes it out onto the balcony we are lost, Felix is lost.

I remember Sri Lanka, before Felix, before Alice died, before Cameron came and lied to me.

In the jungles in the north, where the Tamils live, they teach Varma Kalai, a complex system that includes traditional massage, alternative medicine, yoga, and martial arts. I spent six months there, studying, once upon a time.

My breathing is slow and steady. I know I am blocking Cameron's shot but I can't take the chance this man's finger squeezes as his soul departs, and it's not fair anyway, to put this on Cameron.

This is on me, I brought Cameron into our lives, I set in motion the events that lead to here.

If I had been more trustworthy maybe we wouldn't be here.

This is our son but my ultimate responsibility, I'm stronger than Cameron that way.

There are 108 pressure points on the human body, I can find them all, in the dark.

He doesn't expect it. I'm an unarmed man. I'm a poof. He beat me unconscious two days ago.

My hands were tied then.

I leap forward.

The pointed knuckle of my middle finger hits the pressure point where the radial nerve on the back of the hand branches into the median nerve of the trigger finger. The gun drops, I hear it hit the floor.

I push Felix out of the way.

I can hear Cameron yelling at me to get down.

No, this is mine.

The guy stares at me as I clamp my hands around both sides of the jaw, four fingers digging in under the bone and pulling upwards.

My fingers, strong from years of physio, are unrelenting. He opens his mouth, crying out in agony.

I let go. Pulling my arm back I drive a two knuckle punch into his face at an angle of forty five degrees, hitting the buccal nerve. His eyes roll back in his head as he slumps to the side.

Cameron's shot takes him right between the eyes before he can hit the floor.

Camo

"Snipe, want to play a game?" I stand on the concrete slab balcony and look down at the intense azure rectangle of the pool surrounded by grey slabs in front of the monstrous villa.

Guards are stationed around the perimeter, taking shade where they can.

In the middle of the pool a thin shape like a shark swims lengths.

"Always."

"It's fish in a barrel but you deserve a treat."

"On my way."

I don't wait to see what happens.

I go back inside the room where to my surprise of a husband has our son in his arms. "Let's get out of here."

Felix is clasped against Ethan's body. He's in a fugue state, withdrawn in trauma. It's not the first time. His brain, in instances of extreme stress does this. He was like this when they first found him apparently, trapped in an apartment with his dead mother's body.

He came out of it that time, with love. He will again, I am sure. We know how to deal with it. With love and security.

Through the open window of the balcony I can hear the chopper. As I get to the door of the suite the cracks of gunfire start.

Ethan doesn't even flinch.

He doesn't flinch at the sight of the blood in the water either when we climb into the helicopter that lands on the perimeter. He hands Felix into Snipe's careful grasp and climbs in after him. Then he collapses into a seat, just staring at his son in the arms of yet another killer.

I can't tell Ethan how to feel about all this. I have no idea how he will feel about it. I hope there will be questions about who I am, what I have done, and why I do it. If there are questions that means I will be allowed to answer them.

If there are no questions then chances are I won't be able to be a part of Ethan and Felix's life. I will just be cut out.

I won't blame him, not when what I do has led to this.

I look at Ethan, streaked with sweat and dirt, bruised and hurting but more amazing than I ever thought possible. I hope to hell he will let us try to make it work because if I loved him before I love him a hundred times more now.

The bad shit will always find people like me and my team, it's like we are magnets for trouble. Is it selfish to try and have a normal life when you are like this? Probably, but I'm a selfish man, obviously.

Chapter Ten

Ethan

The private jet is waiting on the tarmac.

I carry Felix again. He seems to be sleeping. His vitals are normal, he doesn't appear to have any injuries, this is all psychological and I've seen it before. I need to get him home, get him warm and safe and wait for him to come out of it. Then I will start to deal with it.

Cameron walks beside me, the others trail behind, giving us space.

"How many?" I ask him.

"How many what?"

"People have you killed?"

"I don't know."

"Why not?

"Counting them is crass and revolting."

Thank heavens for small mercies.

We settle into our seats, I keep Felix pressed against me, he will need the body contact.

I close my eyes, pushing away memories as the plane taxies down the runway, the sound of the engines reminding me how I got here.

Once the pilot says we can undo our seatbelts the Team start to move around the cabin, stripping off gear, checking weapons.

"These guys," I say to Cameron, "They're Handlers aren't they. This is what happened to the Handlers."

"Not all of them," he replies.

"No, but some of them."

"Yes, don't look down on them for it."

"I don't. I'm just amazed they helped with this. They didn't have to."

Cameron looks sad, his eyes far away, "It takes a special kind of monster to care about things the way they do."

The guy who took Felix into the helicopter, Snipe, comes towards me, his expression shy. "I can take him for a bit," he says, "If you want to get changed into something cleaner, have a wash, or something."

There is something almost yearning in his face and he holds his arms out.

"Thank you."

He lifts Felix from my arms and settles into the chair opposite. He cradles Felix so gently. With such tenderness it makes me want to cry, or maybe that's just reaction setting in.

Cameron follows me to the rear of the plane, rummaging through a kit bag and pulling black pants and a clean shirt out. He passes them to me.

"I don't know what will happen next," I say to him because I know he is thinking about it. "I don't know where we go from here."

"You don't have to, you have all the time in the world to figure it out."

"I don't even know if you love me, if you love Felix. I don't know if you can love."

I feel a presence behind me. Something ancient in me senses it, warns me. I feel the hair rise on the back of my neck. I turn to see Blue standing behind me. His face is smooth and handsome, his eyes calm. He blinks at me. "Look at me, I'm harmless," whispers his deviancy but I have seen him. I know.

He leans towards me, whispers in my ear, "He's normal, he's not like me, he loves, trust me, he loves."

I glance at Cameron, he has a strange smile on his face. Almost proud.

"I'm sorry," I start to say to Blue, "I didn't mean to imply..."

I did, but I don't now.

Blue shrugs, "I'm just another kind of human, trying to make it through."

"It's a lot to take in. The killing, the pain. I don't know how to feel about it. I didn't think I would ever face this in my life."

"Turns out you're good at it," Blue says, "Who would have suspected that."

Felix wakes briefly as I make my way back to my seat. He just opens his eyes and looks up at Snipe. "Hey," says Snipe, "You're Dad's are here."

"Good," Felix's voice comes out quiet and rusty.

"Wanna go to them?"

Felix nods and Snipe, so gently, so carefully, sets him on his feet.

I pull him into my arms. He smells dreadful but his warm body is the most precious thing and little boys always smell a little.

I manage to get him to drink something and tenderly wash his face before he yawns and drifts off to sleep.

When he wakes again as we come into land in Washington he seems oblivious to what has happened but I doubt that is the case. He isn't stupid and he has regular therapy where his previous trauma is brought out for him to poke at. Maybe he just thinks this is what life is like, everything sunny until suddenly it's not and you have to do what is necessary to get through.

Maybe life really is like that.

I don't know how I am going to explain this to his therapist but there is no getting around that. Honesty is the watchword.

Cameron comes home with us, for Felix's sake, and we feed him and bath him and tuck him into bed together. He doesn't ask what we were doing on a plane or where we have been. He makes no comment about the state of my face. He listens as we read him a story each and by halfway through the second his eyes are drooping and he drifts off to sleep again.

We leave the door of his room open and Cameron follows me into our bedroom.

It's all so normal. Cameron is back in his usual jeans and tshirt, no sign of combats or guns or kevlar. He sits on the bed with a sigh. "I could sleep for a week."

"Me too."

Suddenly I can't look at him. I am caught in a strange shyness. Like this is the first time we were ever anywhere as intimate as a bedroom.

"Where do you want me to sleep?" he asks.

I look down on my bare feet on the cream coir rug. I rub my toes over it and my skin prickles.

"Ethan." His voice is deeper, more commanding. "Look at me."

I lift my head. I know him and I don't know him. I suddenly find that incredibly hot.

He sees it in my face, because despite it all he still knows me.

"What do you want, Ethan? I can see you want something."

I want my life back. I want my husband back. I want to find a way to let that happen.

His hand reaches for mine and he pulls me towards him. I go, climbing onto his lap, my legs on either side of his thick thighs.

His hand runs slowly up my back, his face is serious looking up at me. I lean down and lick the outline of his lips, my tongue light.

He shivers. Normally that's my reaction.

He wraps an arm around me and lies back, pulling me with him, but gently, his body cushioning mine.

"You are so beautiful. I love you so much." He arranges me on my back, stroking my face.

Slowly he undoes my second hand shirt, and I let him. His touch is featherlight, stroking over my bruises, making the dull ache vanish.

His lips find my nipples, sucking them lightly, and his hand trails down my body to where my cock is pressing hard against my jeans.

Maybe it's true, nearly dying makes you want to live.

Maybe violence makes you horny.

He is gentle, peeling my pants open, sliding his hand into my shorts and cupping my balls, rolling them in his big hands. I moan for more.

My breath is coming in soft pants when he slides down the bed and draws my pants and shorts off. His mouth on my cock is soft at first. He laps me with his tongue, pressing the tip into my hole and then suckling the head.

His lips grow firmer around me and he slides down my length.

I weave my fingers in his short hair, encouraging him to go deeper and he does. I feel my cock hit the back of his throat and the muscle there convulses around me.

I draws off slowly.

"Mind if I take care of myself too?"

I shake my head, wordless, as ever blown away at how much I turn him on.

I watch him slide back down again, enveloping me with his mouth. I can see his arm moving as he jerks himself in time to his mouth on my cock.

I let my head fall back, lost in the suction and the heat and the pleasure that comes from the hard press of his tongue and knowing he got hard without me even touching him.

That thought, more than anything, sends my orgasm spiraling through me.

It's like a warm rushing wave, familiar and beloved and so needed.

I moan quietly through it and I feel Cameron tensing, I see his shoulders curl forward and he pants into my belly as his own orgasm spills over.

Chapter Eleven

Camo

Just for a second, after the orgasm washes through Ethan everything is okay, everything is as it was.

I can smell my husband's well known scent, his skin on mine is familiar and hot, slick with sweat, his eyes looking down into mine are hazy with pleasure.

And then, before I can draw another breath everything changes.

It's like he remembers what has happened and all the anger and the fear and the betrayal come barrelling back. I see it in his face. And I want to break for what I have done and I want to weep because he hasn't really seen me.

"Eth," I say, "Please."

He throws his arm over his eyes and lets out a strangled sound, like a sob.

"Ethan," I say again, "Please look at me. Please don't pull away."

"You need to go Cameron, it's crazy, that was crazy. We can't do that, this, any of it."

I climb to my feet and do up my pants, my come cold on my skin.

Ethan slides off the bed and wriggles into his jeans. The light catches the bruises on his torso.

I don't blame him.

But equally I can't let it go like this. He doesn't know how our future could look. I have to show him.

I have to start talking.

"A guy I know, a Handler, a real hard ass, he told me not so long ago that I liked lying to you." I duck my head at the fury that blazes in Ethan's eyes. Everyone knew before him. I study my boots instead of his face, the laces undone, trailing on the pale wood of the floor. "He was right. I did. But not for the reason he thought."

I remember a night in a bar, with Gray and Nathan and Edwards, the day the Handler system ended. Gray laughed at me when he heard I was getting married and my husband didn't know who I was and what I did.

"I liked lying to you because it meant you and I were separate from that world. We were in our bubble and everything was rosy in the bubble. I liked that. I felt I was getting everything and I could keep everything."

"I wasn't laughing at you, if that's what you think. Nobody was laughing at you. Everyone envied me for that pretty bubble of a life I had.

"Turns out it was no more complete than the other life." I look up at him. "I thought you were sweet and gentle and you wouldn't harm a fly. I thought you wouldn't survive on the other side of my life with the blood and the fear. Turns out I was wrong.

"I have been so wrong I can't even begin to list my mistakes. I was wrong about my team, wrong about myself, so wrong about you." I shake my head, chewing on my lip to try and keep control. "I always thought you were amazing, Ethan, I never realised quite how magnificent you are. You are brave and strong and mentally you wipe the floor with all of us. How I didn't see that I will never know."

His face is unreadable and so I keep talking because talking is the only thing I can do now, and every word has to be the truth.

"I know that what I do is indefensible to you. I know I am a killer. It's the first thing any person would say about me, Camo, killer and liar, real shit human. But you aren't just any person, Eth, you're my husband, you have to look deeper, you can't just take the surface as the only truth about me."

For the first time in my life I open my mouth and I speak my own truth to the man I love.

"I believe in what I do. I know that you can't change the world at the point of a gun. You can't send an army in to make the world a better place, to impose your values on it. What you can do is take a scalpel to the tumours in humanity so the rest can stay healthy. That's what I am, what Stat and Blue, Berk and Snipe are, we're the scalpel. We cut out the tumours so the rest of humanity, the decent, thoughtful, just wanna live their lives, people, get that chance to be heard and make decisions. We're not killing those who disagree with us, we're removing those that have no intention of listening to their own people."

I try to find the words to make him understand.

"We don't go in to start wars or win wars, we go in to try and stop them from happening in the first place. We do what we do so those with integrity get their chance. We're not heroes, but we're more necessary than you could imagine."

I want him to see me. I want him to look below the lies that cover the surface and see me, finally.

"I loved you from the day I met you. At first I lied because it's a habit, but I kept on lying because you really didn't need to know, nobody who isn't part of this needs to know. I wanted your world clean and wholesome and I didn't want to dirty it up with my truth. My truth is dirty. I see now that was wrong, you deserve more than that, you're tougher than I ever imagined and it is no damn wonder I love you so much. You're like me, when the chips are down, you're me and you can handle the truth."

It takes a while for it to sink in, what I am saying.

Ethan isn't stupid and he isn't unfair and if I ask him to look he will look.

This is the court I throw myself on the mercy of, because this court will have mercy.

I watch him process, I want him weigh up what I say, I watch him decide.

He's a good man, my Ethan, he shows mercy.

"If we do this you will never cut me out again. If you are in this I am part of it, no more secrets, no more lies."

I don't know what he means but I will agree to anything at this point.

Chapter Twelve

Ethan

"You're done," I tell Berk. "Just do us all a favour, don't try sparing with Blue until you heal properly."

"I won't," Berk looks shame faced, "I can't believe he dislocated my shoulder on an exercise."

"You caught him on a bad day," I say, "And now they had to take the role without you."

"I could have gone."

"Not ideal." I tell him, turning away to make some notes on his therapy records. "You could have compromised them."

"Are they on the way back?" Berk puts on his shirt, his movements far less stiff than they were before.

"Yes, should be back in a couple of hours." Camo and the team are in Hawaii, lucky assholes, retrieving a whistleblower with information about a backdoor program in satellite technology coming out of Taipei. They are making him disappear and relocating him. They have been gone two weeks. I can't wait for them to come home.

"Are you coming over this weekend?" I ask Berk.

"No, going firewalking."

"Of course you are."

He grins at me, his teeth very white in the thick black of his beard.

"If you decide to change your mind we're having a bbq on Saturday."

Bbq's at the farm are not a weekly thing but I'm trying to make it more normal for all of us.

Camo and I have our own house here now. It's secure, behind the walls of the farm, but more than that it makes sense for Felix and for the team and for me.

I split my time between my practice in town and working on the team who seem to have rather more injuries than they admitted to in the past. Felix has a group of male role models who adore him and who are, like him, living with their pasts, silently and steadily.

I was wrong about a lot of things. I was wrong to think my husband didn't love me because of his lies or his job, he was incorrect in his assumptions, but he truly does love me.

Love requires that you look at more than the surface. It requires that your vision be holistic, you look at the whole thing, the whole person.

Will I always agree with the roles they take? No.

Will I have sleepless nights when he is away? Yes.

But that's life, we don't always agree with those we love, but we have to listen to them and then decide.

None of us are normal, I have a son who descends into a figure state if you frighten him enough. I have a husband who kills. I now have friends who don't feel what I feel but who try to understand it anyway.

I know I can kill too, for the right reason - morality is in the reason.

I'm not what I was but I'm learning who I am.

Camo has changed. I have changed. I think the team is changing too, as much as they can, as much as they are able, slowly but surely.

Edwards sticks his head around the door of my treatment room. "They just landed," he says, "Want to go home and do the husband thing?"

I grin at him. "Hell yes!"

Felix is staying with a friend tonight. I need to go and change the sheets. Dark grey ones I think. I look good against dark grey.

My predator husband is coming home to play.

And if he is all alpha'd out then I am pretty sure I can call on some of my own alphaness to make it another memorable homecoming..

Epilogue

Blue

The door to his house unlocks with a keycode.

There is a scrabble of claws on wood and a deep bark as he pushes the door open.

"Hey, Trans." He falls to his knees and pulls the dog into his arms. It licks his face, long tongue stropping. "Glad to see me?"

The dog barks, excited.

He climbs to his feet, leaving his pack on the floor, toeing off his shoes and padding into the kitchen on socked feet.

The dog follows him, pressed against his leg.

"That was quite the trip," he says to the dog, "Some interesting deaths, some unique observations, I look forward to writing them up."

Death fascinates Blue, it always did, the biology of it, the inability to see exactly what happens. He has studied the mechanics of it, the electricity and the impulse of it, and yet he is still blind to the reality of it.

He and they discussed it endlessly, in their time together, speculating, considering, wondering. He has seen more of it since they went, but it's not the same without them, the fascination is not so delightful any more.

It's hard for him to even think their name. That's why he got Trans, the dog, why he called it Trans.

Not that he should have a dog, he's not supposed to have animals, not really, because he doesn't relate to them. They are in danger with him, he's a psychopath. But he looks after Trans and Trans, in return, gives him something that is gone, but that was there once.

The thoughts, which have veered so close to where they should not go, shift back towards the dog and he makes the conscious effort to touch it, stroke it, give it what it's packmate should offer.

It took Trans a long time to warm to him. Even as a puppy the dog was naturally mistrustful of him. He doesn't smell quite right to animals. They sometimes sense what he is. But because he had the discipline, and the training had been so good, and the fake it until you make it attitude was so ingrained, eventually even the primal in the animal gave in.

It loves him.

He doesn't love it. He doesn't know what love was.

He has a memory of something that the word label could be attached to but...

He bends and hugs the dog again, his arms tightening around it, the warm body, the soft hair, dark and silky.

Trans lays his long elegant muzzle on Indie's shoulder, his whiskers tickling Indie's skin. Indie breathes through the memory, lets it rise up and then drift back down through the layers of his mind when he fails to look at it.

"Come on," he says to Trans, "Let's go for a run."

The scrabble of excitement that causes leaves him with claw marks across his belly.

He remembers the look on the kids face, Camo's kid, Felix, when he interacts with his fathers. Often he doesn't say anything but the expressions run like water across his face, swift and sure, natural and pure.

They speak volumes to one trained to look.

Indie will never be like that. He isn't made that way. That doesn't stop him from being glad that the boy gets to experience them, and it gives him something to continually learn from.

"Appreciation doesn't require reciprocation, just respect." That was what Gray had told him. Years ago. "You don't need to feel it, you just know they do, and you respect that in them. Then, when you do feel something, you treat it for what it is, something to be profoundly grateful for."

Gray taught him a lot about being. After. When it looked like he would go the wrong way.

Gray taught him and threatened him and kicked his ass and fought him when he needed to hurt.

Nathan had never let him down, not as a child, not as a man. He always put him in the place he needed to be, with the resources that could help him.

Indie pulls on his running shoes and catches up with Trans who is sitting bolt upright at the front door, radiating obedient dog vibes, quivering with them.

Just for a second Indie wonders what they looked like inside the dog's brain, all strung tight. Does the obedience form wires in his brain? Could he see them if he looked inside?

He pushes the errant impulse away. Wishes he had someone to discuss the concept with.

He ruffles the hair on Trans' head. "It's gonna be wet," he said, and Trans barks, uncaring and keen.

Indi zips up his windproof hoodie and opens the door.

He runs until he can't think, and Trans paces beside him, down wet slick sidewalk and across puddled blacktop lit with neon, from lamp lit circle to lamp lit circle down sleeping streets.

If another Trans, ghostly and fleet of foot, keeps pace with them through the night, he chooses not to look. There is no point, he is always disappointed when he tries to catch a glimpse.

Monsters don't get to live happily ever after.

Blue's story will be told in Blueprint, Book Two of The Teams

The Teams Series

Camouflage - CAMO - The Leader - Alpha - Accomplished Liar
Blueprint - BLUE (Indigo) - The Arranger – Psychopath - Utterly Lost
Static - STAT - The Communicator - Extrovert - Drowning in Secrets
Bullseye - SNIPE - The Sniper - Focussed - Boiling inside
Berserk - BERK - The Enforcer - Titan - Totally Terrified

More About Romilly King

Hi, I hope you enjoyed this book. If you did you may want to check out my other novels (and assorted freebies) by visiting my website. All books can be bought direct, at a discount, on my website.

Romilly King Website[1]

Thanks for reading!

Rom

---

1.   http://www.romillyking.com

Don't miss out!

Visit the website below and you can sign up to receive emails whenever Romilly King publishes a new book. There's no charge and no obligation.

https://books2read.com/r/B-A-JNCL-HTVTB

BOOKS 2 READ

Connecting independent readers to independent writers.

Milton Keynes UK
Ingram Content Group UK Ltd.
UKHW041815060923
428148UK00001B/41